Kharishma

A Novel

Jenny L. R. Nay

Leuchalad Press

Published in the United States by *Leuchalad Press*

ISBN 978-0-615-97401-9 (paperback)

Leuchalad Press

leuchaladpress@gmail.com

For Ryan,
who never doubted

Prologue ✎

The pain began as a small murmur, a tug really, that was now so great it filled every pore in her trembling body. It came without warning, as if a switch had turned it on. *How did I get here?* she wondered. *This was not the plan to die here alone.* A high scream escaped her mouth and immediately shame filled her heart. She wanted to let it happen with dignity, without weakness; she tried hard to swallow the urge to cry out. Her wild hands could not be calmed as they tussled with her dark hair, fingers ringing and tugging, again and again. Some kind of movement, any movement, helped her cope with the awful surge that consumed her.

Her lower half was almost paralyzed, as her insides seemed to be forcing themselves out; bone and muscle, once devoted, now combined against her.

The cold, unfeeling sheet that covered her naked body mingled with beading sweat and clung to her, creating almost a new layer of skin. Her teeth were clenched, constraining her breath. She needed life-giving air and knew she wouldn't last much longer without it, but she couldn't relax her chest long enough to receive it. Every muscle was tight like a rubber band, pulled nearly to the point of breaking yet, finally, her chest gave in, heaving and sucking in needed breaths. Still, her once limber, pink, body now appeared pale and statuesque. Feeling anything against her skin tormented her and she wished to be suspended in space where nothing could touch her. Even the soft glow of a nearby lamp irritated her.

With thirst on her tongue, she grappled for sweet memories and blissful thoughts, the only things the pain couldn't reach. For a mere moment, her thoughts conquered the pain and she hid from the light's invasiveness. She fell far into her mind's refuge dark, safe, away from her reality. She could see and feel nothing, as if her existence had disappeared. It was peaceful and unknown. She curled up there and rested for a moment until a voice, distant, yet sure, pulled her back from her hazy nowhere. The encouraging tone called her by name in a futile attempt to grant her peace. She responded indignantly to it somewhere deep in her brain; the kindness of the voice only patronized her and she tried to push it away. However, the voice was unrelenting. Its power drew her from her mind's safety and she was once again entangled in a flood of anguish, searching for relief.

Her grip tightened to the bed as she begged for help, knowing full well none would come. Suddenly, an unfamiliar urge to finish what she had set in motion frenzied within her. She needed to get it out of her. It was time. Gathering every piece of herself, she pushed from deep inside, unsure of what would happen next, only knowing the urge could not be denied. Pausing for a breath, she feared she had no more energy in her to continue. Yet, when the surge returned, she gathered herself once more, attempting to physically thrust the urge away. In a sweet instant, her whole being exhaled, and as suddenly as it had come, the suffering was over and indescribable relief now took its place.

Lying at her feet was a new life, purple, wet and still. Breathing heavily, she wished to hear its breath as well and slid her shaking hands under the tiny someone. It was covered in warmth, eyes closed, arms and legs folded gently into itself. She was calm as she held the fragile being in her hands and laid it gently on her chest before lifting its arm and massaging its torso with her fingers, trying to help it breathe. Instinctively and naturally, the song from her childhood rose from her lips and she sang a soothing lullaby to the little one. Whispers of lilacs, roses, soft breezes and love all danced around them in the form of an ancient song. Silence, anticipation, and hope lingered within her as she watched and waited. At last there was a breath, a movement, and, finally, a cry.

Chapter One ✎

With sluggish eyes and ringing ears, Khari sat at the edge of her bed just as the grey light slowly emerged through the double-paned window. The dream she had just awakened from brought a rush of emotions and a familiar ache grew within her. She wanted to stay ignorant of what was occurring, but there was no denying that a stir and a weight were growing deep in her heart. The dream, thick and shadowy, had come again, the third night straight. She sensed that it was more than just created pictures in her mind as so many dreams are, but that it had come with purpose, directly seeking her out. It had felt so real.

Hoping to make the spreading ache disappear and bring back the carefree emotions she had felt the previous evening, she shook her head and tried to focus on the music and dancing. It had been an amazing night of electric fun that she had not wanted to end. However, concentrating on the revelry didn't help and the sting of the haunting whispers and fiery shadows stuck. She tried switching thoughts to the day ahead, knowing it would be her last in London before returning home. Her suitcase lay open and empty against the wall. She glanced its way, admitting that she couldn't bring herself to fill it. Each day she hoped that something, anything, would transpire to keep her from returning. Her thoughts of home only strengthened the emotions of the startling dream and she was left enveloped in its depth.

Lightly combing her hands through her thick, dark hair, she squinted her eyes toward the now brightened window, and listened for signs of the London streets beginning their day. The familiar trickle of cars began emerging and then fading down the avenue. She concentrated on them, feeling more grounded by the moment, until a familiar roar caught her attention and finally released her from the dark emotions.

"Not again!" she muttered as she sprang out of bed tangled in the white quilt that clung to her legs and sent her crashing into the nearby wall. A starry grey filled her eyes from stirring too quickly from her sedentary state and she stayed still for a moment to regain her sight. When it finally returned, she wiggled her legs and freed herself from her entanglement with a quick hop over the restrictive quilt.

"I always forget!" she grumbled out loud.

She quickly grabbed the nearest piece of clothing, a green dress she had left on the floor the night before, and pulled it over her head. She zipped it, and, ignoring her shoes tucked in the corner, fled the comfort of her room.

Racing down the wooden stairs, missing half of them on her way, she swung open the front door and ran to the side of the house where the garbage can silently waited. She had missed last week's pick up and couldn't stand the thought of smelling Chinese food leftovers one more day, or hearing the exhausted complaints from the neighbors who shared the otherwise pristine courtyard.

Grabbing the skimpy handle of the silver can, Khari lugged it over the cement and through the iron gate that surrounded the white Victorian home. The can bit at her heels as it scratched and clanged its way after her, forcing a tiny hop to accompany each quick step. Feeling a satisfied exhaustion, as if winning an important race, Khari stepped back to catch her breath and gently lifted her shoulder length hair from her neck as she watched the nearing truck. Clumsily moaning under its weight, the truck grabbed the can with its large metal arm and dumped the contents into the gaping mouth on its side. Somehow Khari instantly felt lighter and she relished the sensation.

"Thanks Marty!" she yelled over the noise of the truck as it pulled away, dreadfully aware of her foolish appearance—hunched over and out of breath wrestling a garbage can in a party dress. Khari knew it was odd for a person to know the first name of their garbage collector, but she had gotten to know him over the past few months. They had a rendezvous every Friday morning— garbage day.

"Catch ya next week!" he yelled back in his playful voice. His bald head reflected the new light as he pulled away and around the corner.

"Same place, same time," Khari muttered under her breath, yanking the now nimble can onto the sidewalk. She realized too late that there would not be a next time and wished she had said some sort of good-bye. Instead, she watched the truck disappear slowly around the corner.

She grabbed the handle of the now empty can and dragged it back to its place beside the house, grateful for its new lightness. There was a strange sadness in Khari at the thought of never struggling with the thing again, as if she was abandoning a difficult pet to the hands of another. As the sound of the truck faded completely in the distance, Khari took a deep breath and one last glance down the road before tiptoeing across the cement courtyard, being careful not to step on any of the loose rocks that she had felt stabbing her feet before.

Her thoughts turned once again to her vivid nightmare and the strong emotions it had evoked. What was happening to her? She had left home with the hope that the constant pull in her middle would disappear and it mostly had. It was a feeling she had felt her entire life and that had plagued her with its sting. She never understood what it meant and she just wanted to be rid of it. Could these dreams be part of what she tried to escape?

She stood up straight and peered around the courtyard taking in deep breaths in an attempt to soothe her trouble mind. As she did she noticed a single bee sitting silently atop the cement post at the foot of the stairs. The insect felt strangely out of place. It should have been busy among the flowers as other bees were that morning. As Khari stared, it seemed to be watching her and so she moved gingerly past to see if it would follow, but it didn't. The bee's stillness made her curious and so she turned and neared it, standing close enough to see the curvature of the deep black lines across its body and the tiny spikes on its thin legs. She gazed at it, waiting for it to stir, but it didn't move. Wanting to test it, she gave it a soft puff of breath across its back, but besides the tiny twitch of the air touching its wings, it stayed still.

Khari felt a bit irrational wasting time with the small creature and began backing up to the stairs when, without warning, a pulse of wind pushed its way across the courtyard and enveloped her. There were soft voices hidden within its folds. Khari glanced around, searching the sidewalks and surrounding buildings for the source of whispers, even glimpsing toward the stationary bee, yet there was no sign of where they had come from.

Khari was startled and confused. She wanted to run inside and escape the strange eruption when within the new rush of wind a surprise of loveliness passed through her. All of her fear and reluctance faded away and she could feel the medley of the cool cement underfoot, the delicate morning sun, and a breeze, soft and sweet, as if blown from the mouth of a kind god. Her mind and heart were lost completely, taken from the city of cement and glass and left on the doorstep of her homeland. The trees, lakes, rivers and surrounding farms were a world away, but appeared as real as a painting on a wall before her. After almost a year of living in London, she could now make out every stunning detail of her Oregon territory.

A distant memory called, and she turned out of herself to listen. The gentle wind swirled around her and carried the small bee on its invisible skin, ushering it swiftly to Khari's ear. The tiny creature took a sudden landing on her bronzed cheek and seemed to march out a circle formation near her tightened jaw before it became still.

In Khari's dreamy state, she knew the bee was there, yet she didn't startle. She only listened, curious for a sound. Her dark eyes tightened, as if to amplify her hearing, while a faint memory of days past flickered in her mind and she recalled some connection to the tiny animal, even though she was unsure how. Everything she had once pushed away, she welcomed back to her. She couldn't resist. She strained her ears and slowed her breath, scared that any movement would force the bee away. But it didn't stir and only breathed along with her. She waited, intently hoping for more. With the rising of the wind, shoving and wrenching around her, a low drone sounded, slow, and timid, until, in one small instant, it was over.

Even though what had brushed against her cheek had not been harsh, it seemed to throb as it ripped her from her peace. The bee tumbled away unharmed on the breeze, as did Khari from her musing.

She turned, ready to scold the nuisance that had parted them, only to see Simon standing next to her.

"I just saved you from a *very* swollen face," he said in a deep British accent.

He was standing with a rolled newspaper in one hand, slapping it into the palm of the other, the title *SUN* showing across the front. He had obviously been awake long before Khari, his hair sleek and stylish as if he was ready for a photo shoot. His light yellow button-up shirt sleeves, loosely rolled to the middle of his forearms, seemed to be deliberately chosen to harmonize with his sandy colored hair. The shirt was tucked neatly into his cool colored slacks, complemented with a black belt. His matching black leather shoes, shiny enough she could see her reflection, finished off his impressive ensemble. Khari imagined a clothing store mannequin naked in some nearby window.

Simon had been the first to befriend Khari when she arrived in London. Just eighteen, she was given the opportunity to work with Elise, an acquaintance of her mother's who lived the majority of the time in Oregon and part of her time in England. Elise was a clothing expert in the fashion world and her work brought her to London during peak fashion season. Khari's mother had arranged for Khari to go with Elise and learn in London as Khari had always been drawn to art. Her mother saw it as a wonderful opportunity for her to strengthen her artistic talents. Even though Elise was never around, she had placed Khari with a job assisting any designers with their clothing lines. Which really meant Khari got to take care of loose ends or undesirable tasks. What her mother didn't realize, and what would have caused her to worry, was that most of the time Elise was traveling around Europe leaving Khari on her own. Even her first day as an apprentice was spent without anyone familiar by her side. Luckily, Simon had stepped in.

Though Simon was the same age as Khari, he held an important position with the lead coordinator over fashion events. Having grown up in the industry, the only child of famous fashion proprietors, he had a wealth of experience. He befriended Khari her first time assisting a show as she was making her way through a sea of frantic models and designers with her arms stacked with accessories prepared for the runway. With only ten minutes until show time, he guided her to the backstage. He helped Khari feel comfortable, sharing with her vital gossip, and giving her much needed advice. A while after becoming good friends, they began dating. However, in this moment, standing stunned in the courtyard, Khari was not in the mood to see him. His timing could not be worse. She tried to hide her annoyance with a gentle smile.

"What are you doing here?" she asked while turning slightly to look for the bee.

"Couldn't you feel that menacing bee on your face? I was trying to help you. A thank you would suffice," he said in defense to her distressed stare.

Khari tucked her hair behind her ear feeling awkward and somewhat lost.

"I was fine. It wasn't going to hurt me...I..." She could tell by the look on his face he was confused by her defense of the creature and so she stopped. "You just scared me," her voice faded away, as she said it. However, her hazel eyes, more green than brown from the emerald dress she wore, couldn't hide their intensity.

"I completely apologize. I didn't mean to scare you," he said in a voice dipped in both cleverness and appease. He placed his hands on her shoulders and looked her in the eye.

"I called your name several times and you didn't hear me. I saw the thing on your cheek and thought you were sleepwalking or something. What were you doing with your eyes closed? Why couldn't you hear me?"

Khari wasn't sure how to respond to a question she didn't know the answer to.

"I guess I was just enjoying the sun on my face," she finally replied, trying to lose his gaze.

"Well, I can see that you are either planning on humiliating yourself by wearing the same dress you wore last night, or you were trying to spoil an expensive Shanista original by wearing it as a night- gown," he said smiling, obviously humored by his gentle mockery.

His comment brought her back and she started to recap in her mind what had happened in the last five minutes. She was now mortified that he had seen her in her current condition. Had she heard something from the bee? It passed so quickly she couldn't recall. Ready for the conversation to end, Khari backed up toward the front steps.

"Don't worry, just give me thirty minutes and I'll be completely presentable for the show. Come in and wait," she offered, trying to smooth over the awkwardness.

Regretting the whole situation, her face flushed, as she took several timid steps up the stairs.

Simon walked backwards while throwing a hitchhiker thumb over his shoulder. "I'll be back then. I need to pick up the programs. Please be ready. We cannot be late."

Khari ran up the steps and pushed through the door. She hoped the rest of the day would not be as difficult as the morning had been and tried to shake the intense emotions that had overwhelmed her. She was desperate to stay in London and hoped that something would happen, even though she wasn't sure staying would help anymore.

Chapter Two ✥

Simon's flawless punctuality hurried Khari along and twenty-nine minutes later they made their way through the posh streets of London. Khari left her hair down, and wore a yellow dress that she had saved from last season's throwaway pile, which was still like new. It was Friday, which meant less commotion in the streets, leaving the sound of her black-strapped heels to click loudly against the sidewalk as they made their way toward the venue. Khari held Simon's arm lightly to help her balance.

Not only was Simon handsome and charismatic, he never asked personal questions, which helped Khari in her effort to forget her past—a past she wasn't ready to think about, much less divulge to anyone. She never inquired about the details of his life either. They just enjoyed the now, not concerned about what was in front of them or behind.

As they walked, Simon concentrated quietly on the show's programs in his hands, intensely mulling over each word. His obsession with doing his job well was the reason he frequently felt so distant and Khari knew he would not want to be disturbed. His cell phone inside of his front shirt pocket began to sing and they paused in front of a bus stop near their destination so he could take the call.

She stepped several paces away to give him privacy, or at least to help her not hear his sharp commands to whoever was on the other side of the call. She shivered at a bit of cool spring air that rushed across her bare arms. The gentle touch of the season was a greater companion to her now than Simon. She took in a deep breath and caught the crisp smell of London, a mix of curry, blossoms and pollution. Somehow the medley worked.

She watched the street as a man and woman appeared from around the corner. The man walked calmly with his arm around the woman's shoulders trying to steady her as she stumbled along. She was well dressed, blonde, wearing slacks and a flowered top finished with a string of pearls. He carried what Khari guessed was the woman's purse and her heels in his other hand.

The man was tall, dark haired, and wore gray sweats. He appeared to be bringing the woman home from her drinking revelry. She walked along barefoot, giggling, and unable to stand up straight on her own, her lost eyes searched for a permanent direction as she attempted to caress the man's unshaven face. The expression on the man was stoic and weary as if he was exhausted from caring for her. Khari looked away as they passed. For some reason his uneasy gaze reminded her of a person she had known since childhood. He too held that same look upon his face the last time she had seen him. A familiar pain entered Khari's chest, a taste of a sentiment she thought was gone. As Simon finished his call and they made their way toward the park, she pushed the thoughts away and held tight to the day ahead of her.

The tinkling of crystal and soft music playing amongst the trees replaced the rush of cars when they stepped from the street and into the park. Saying good-bye to Simon, Khari immediately started for the back tent where she was to help the designers fit the models into their clothing. Although Khari and Simon had been dating for several months, Simon didn't think it was appropriate to tell anyone, so they remained discrete during events.

Simon began placing the freshly printed programs to the side of each plate on the large round tables. The tables were covered in white and yellow cloths and topped with bright yellow umbrellas to guard against the heat of the sun. Surrounding a long glass catwalk, they were arranged in an orderly fashion, looking like sunflowers popping from a garden.

While some of the waiters refined the tables with necessary silver and glasses, several others arranged flawless white chocolate swan centerpieces and fixed napkins folded in the same graceful form atop the plates. The swan theme was woven into every inch of the spring fashion show. Real swans waddled through the party while their ice twins graced the buffet tables. Khari noticed the now empty pond and wondered if the swans were not brought in, but had decided to attend, waddling up the hill to the festivities. Khari chuckled at the idea of them crashing a fashion show. The warmth of the late morning sun began to chase the chill from Khari's skin and its supple light reflected off the shiny plates and silver forks, as if the sun had been shattered and tossed across them.

A few guests began to trickle in, more than likely to start eating the luscious food Khari could now smell. The scent of the catered lunch dropped a boulder of hunger into her stomach and reminded her that she had forgotten breakfast. She headed toward the food, hoping to grab one finger sandwich on her way to the tent. As she reached the buffet table, Khari felt Simon watching her while he discussed some wilting flower arrangements with the florist. She was suddenly filled with embarrassment from bypassing her waiting job to ease her hunger and although she could not see his face, she imagined Simon's judgmental eyebrow raised in an attempt to discipline her. Simon believed in eating moderately to retain a healthy figure and mind. His chiseled muscles were retained by daily protein shakes and a strict diet of veggies and fish. When Khari and Simon dined together, she endured the offhand lectures and was always amazed at his ordering routine, choreographed down to the crumb. Just another piece to his perfect puzzle.

Khari, on the other hand, enjoyed food. Growing up,

her mother, who had always worked as a caterer, often made new dishes and baked goods from various parts of the world, encouraging Khari to gain an appreciation for different cultures. Khari savored the novel flavors and enjoyed the cultural discoveries food brought. To her, food was a delightful celebration. Khari turned slightly to look at Simon. He smiled and waved. Khari grinned and waved back as she bit into the sandwich and made her way toward the large white tent.

Once inside, a flood of noise and bustle rushed over Khari. Going from the calm outside to the chaos within the tent, was as abrupt as leaving frigid cold and entering a hot sauna. Since it was a spring showcase for a few of the top designers, there was more mayhem and a lot more people than Khari had experienced during a single designer's show.

Everyone was busy, each at their own stations. Models were enduring the grooming process that, to Khari, seemed more like torture. The thick make-up was applied, and then their hair was pulled, ratted, stretched and almost burned by the different contraptions forced upon them by the stylists. A few models with hair and make-up finished, were now enduring their fittings as they were crammed and pulled into their clothes as one would squeeze sausage into its casing. Several were then sewn or glued in tight at the seams.

Floating among the smells of hot glue, hairspray and perfume, Khari caught a whiff of singed hair. The instant the scent reached her, a shrill from a far corner chair silenced the persistent chatter and everyone stared in its direction. A lanky short-haired brunette was cursing in a language Khari recognized as Greek, while holding a small strand of hair ready to fling into the face of a hair stylist. With the flat iron still in his hand, the stylist's juvenile face looked like he was going to be sick. After hard stares from the crowd, the howling woman marched her way through the exit before everyone returned to their work.

Khari began making her way through the swarm, trying to get to Leif, the designer she was assigned to, when a voice came from behind.

"Khari! Khari!" called Jacques in a French accent so thick, it sounded more like he was trying to clear his throat. He followed close behind her, waving his arms above his head since his short height made him disappear entirely amongst the tall girls.

"We have need of you," he said, grabbing Khari by the arm, ushering her back through the path he had cleared. She tried to explain where she was supposed to be, but she could barely hear her own voice. She was annoyed at his forcefulness and was ready to wrestle herself away from his grasp when they finally stopped in front of the dressing room prepared from hanging red cloth.

"What's wrong Jacques?" Khari asked, hoping he would detect the annoyance in her voice.

"Oh Khari! The luscious Miangalo has fallen ill and we have not a person to wear the white dress that Launa has prepared. It is still hanging in the dressing room when it should have been hanging around a warm body a half-an-hour ago."

One hand seemed to be glued to his forehead, the other nervously stroked his unimpressive goatee as he paced in the corner. His thick, black-rimmed glasses intensified his worried eyes to the point of bulging much like fish eyes through a curved glass water bowl.

Khari understood the reason for his anxiety. The New York designer Launa was known for firing people on the spot for merely sneezing. She expected perfection as if every individual naturally encompassed the quality. Luckily, Khari never had to assist her in anything, but was oftentimes around when she was dominating the scene and ordering Jacques and her other assistants around. She was surly and blunt, and could be pleasant if you pleased her, yet it was impossible to know how. Khari thought her similar to a stalk of rhubarb—naturally bitter, possibly sweet with a lot of added sugar, and fully toxic if used the wrong way.

Khari began to back away. She didn't want to seem heartless, Jacques had always been kind to her, but she was expected on the other end of the tent to help Lief put the finishing touches on his clothing and she didn't want to be late.

"Jacques, I'm sorry, but I'm not assigned to Launa. Leif is waiting at his station for me to help."

"Oh, S'il vous plait Khari. You are the only one not designated an ensemble who is even close to Miangalo's size. For me, you must wear the dress. You must show the dress!"

Khari turned and looked harder at him, trying to

understand. A drop of moisture rolled down Jacques' cheek and Khari hoped it had left his sweaty brow and not his worried eye.

"What are you saying Jacques?" Khari wished for a response contrary to the one she was expecting.

"I need you to model." He pronounced his words slowly making sure he was understood.

Those words Khari comprehended completely, and her body began to respond like a mouse before a snake.

"Oh no....I can't…I'm not…"

"Je Sais, I know, but we have no choice. My cheri please get dressed."

He urged Khari through the curtain into what felt like an oversized locker and poked his head in before speaking more rapidly than she had ever heard.

"I will go and explain to Leif. He owes me a favor, and will help me out. You will have to get hair and make-up *after* you are dressed."

With that, he closed the curtain and began yelling for Leif on his way down the tent.

Khari froze and tried to process what was happening. She stared at the white dress hanging in front of her, admiring its clean lines. She had never worn the elegant clothing she helped the models into, though she had always wanted to.

She laid her black handbag on the floor, removed her dress and heels and placed them inside. Taking a deep breath, she ran the white dress through her fingers. Its ruched empire waist and capped shoulders were lined with lavender lace while the bottom was layered in chiffon that gently swayed at her touch. She recognized the design as one of Launa's that she had seen in the studio and felt nervous and excited to try it on. In that moment, she felt like a servant playing dress-up in the closet of a princess.

She removed it from its hanger and slipped it over her head. It swayed as the bottom fell to her feet. She was sure it was not meant to fall so low, but she was somewhat shorter than the lanky Miangalo. The dress formed immediately to her body and she worried it would be too tight to fasten. She was now grateful for not eating more this morning. Even without a mirror, Khari instantly felt elegant as it brushed against her skin.

Can I really pull this off? Khari wondered.

Anxious to find out, Khari poked her head through the curtain and began searching for someone to tell her where to go next, or to at least to fasten her dress. It was difficult to sort through the cluster of people as she searched for Jacques. She was about to tuck back inside and hide when she caught sight of eyes staring at her from a clearing of people. Khari's stomach filled with knots.

Oh no, she thought. *Please don't be looking at me.*

It was Cecile. She was a hair and make-up *aesthete*, as she insisted on being called, and every time she and Khari were in the same room, it seemed that Cecile was staring at her, even when she was in the middle of an argument with others. Which, from Khari's point of view, occurred quite often.

Maybe she wasn't looking at me, Khari hoped. She

continued perusing the room wishing that when she looked that way again Cecile would be gone. Cecile's eyes again met Khari's, this time accompanied with a quick hand gesture to come. After a personal pep talk and an attempt at a polite smile, Khari left her bag, closed the curtain and passed reluctantly to Cecile's chair.

At Cecile's station, instead of a mirror, several hair irons and a blow dryer hung in its place. Khari was disappointed; she was hoping to get a glimpse of what she looked like in the dress.

"I have been given charge over you. Please sit," Cecile said motioning to the styling chair before her. Khari didn't recognize Cecile's accent, but its roughness and depth seemed to age her ten years when she spoke. Her face was attractive, yet stern, and Khari wondered if she was even more annoyed than usual at being assigned to take care of her.

Khari sat in the chair and hoped she could be calm enough to appear pleasant. Cecile took Khari's chin and raised her head up, examining her face closely.

"Your skin is creamy like caramel. Where does this come from?"

Khari could smell black licorice on Cecile's breath as she talked.

"My father was white, and my mom is Native American."

"Well that explains it. I have often wondered your birth. You are different from the other girls. You take more after your mother. She must have strong blood. Well, I know exactly what to do with your delicate

23

features," she said while brushing Khari's face with powder. "Strange, you speak of your father in the past, but your mother in the present. Your father is gone?"

Even though she never minded speaking of her father, Khari was taken aback by her direct questions and tried not to stumble over her answer as she gazed at her hands. She scratched at her nail polish that was beginning to chip away.

"Yes. My father died before I was born. My mother raised me alone." Khari hoped that was the last of her questions and wished her mother was here on this strange day.

"Well, thank the rocks in the ground and the clouds in the sky for mothers, no?" Cecile said, as she leaned in to apply Khari's makeup. Khari was instantly uncomfortable at their closeness, and tried to focus on Cecile's frizzy hair, instead of making eye contact.

They were both silent as Khari's hair, make-up and nails were done. It wasn't a usual practice for the hands and the feet to receive such attention, but it was a necessity today since the models were walking bare foot to show off the new spring line. It was a relief to Khari that she didn't have to tackle the catwalk for the first time in heels.

Khari enjoyed the quiet pampering, surprised that she wasn't being inundated with the usual harshness. Cecile was giving her a gentle look with soft curls and lighter make-up than some of the other models endured. It calmed Khari, helping her forget that the runway was next. After finishing Khari's makeup, Cecile, without a smile, mumbled various foreign words in satisfaction as she leaned back to admire her work.

"You are ready. Please wait while I spray."

As Cecile lifted the hairspray can from her small table, Khari caught a glimpse of a familiar black speck lying amongst the array of beauty products. She instantly recognized what it was—a lifeless honeybee. Cecile saw it too and was about to brush the thing away when Khari quickly reached for the bee and without hesitation, lifted it gingerly between her fingers.

It had curled from its death, head nearly touching its bottom, wings in disarray and motionless. Khari could see its tiny black eyes, the only part of it that held no sign of its demise. She stared into them hoping the bee would rouse and fly away. She waited, but it lay silent. Sorrowfully, she knew it would not move again.

Khari felt a subtle pain for the creature rise within her, connecting her to it. She placed the bee in the palm of her hand and instinctively began to hum, a hum so soft it was almost a whisper. She knew the song from her childhood. Her mother had sung it to her hundreds of times. Its rhythm and flow grew stronger within her and her whispers got louder as well. The stirring inside of Khari made her tremble with confusion and she nearly dropped the creature to the ground.

"A bee huh? It must have made its way inside the tent." Cecile stood beside Khari looking into her hand. "Is it dead?"

"Um…yes…I think so," Khari answered, stumbling on her words. She was unable to remove her gaze from the insect.

"They are dying you know…the honey bees." Cecile motioned to Khari's hand.

"I heard that. Does anyone know why?"

"There are theories why, but they haven't figured it out yet. Every country is trying to solve the great mystery. It is strange, no?"

Khari couldn't answer. Somewhere inside her she felt like she should know why. She felt a whisper, a prompting from within that *she* knew, but how could she? She shook her head as if trying to clear it and walked the bee out of the tent where she was alone and laid it softly in the grass.

"Wait Khari! You are not supposed to leave the tent. And your dress is not fastened!" Cecile called after her as she followed Khari from the tent finally standing next to her. She looked over Khari's shoulder. "What are you doing?"

"I just thought he needed a better spot to lie than under our feet," Khari mumbled.

They were quiet for a moment until an authoritative voice that Khari instantly recognized as Launa's, came abruptly from behind.

"Is anybody going to fasten the girl up?"

Launa stood over them, with her latest choice of red hair radiating from her small head. Her straight short hair, bangs included, framed her glaring eyes and attractive pointy face. Her hair color was ever changing and one never knew what shade to expect. This aspect of surprise matched her personality perfectly. With her new flaming hair and her exceptionally skinny body, Launa looked like she had fallen from a matchstick box and would ignite at any moment.

Launa stood there with a look of disgust on her face. Khari imagined she had not reacted well to the news that they needed Khari to wear her precious dress. Launa's entourage hurried to Khari's back, pulling at the dress's opening. Khari held her breath, relieved it fit as they zipped it to the top.

Jacques stood directly behind Launa, draped with the same dreaded look he had earlier. She knew she had made a mistake. Launa wouldn't have left the tent just to see her.

"Is there a legitimate reason that you are trying to ruin the element of surprise by walking out of the tent and into the view of hundreds of people?"

Khari thought that any excuse she gave the woman would not be adequate, so she kept her mouth closed.

"If you were a real model and had a clue about what you were supposed to be doing, I would throw you out of here at once. But since you are ignorant to show procedure I will let it slide. Jacques explained our need to use you, the dress must be debuted, and so I expect you to wear it proudly and not to botch things up."

Actually, Khari knew full well that a model never enters the view of the audience until they appear on the catwalk. She paid attention to details while working with them, but it seemed safer to let Launa think otherwise.

Launa stepped toward Khari and arranged pieces of the dress, and tried several strands of Khari's hair behind her ear, tucking and removing it several times until she finally appeared satisfied. Up close, Khari could see the make-up covered lines that were beginning to grace Launa's face, mostly around her down turned mouth. The black turtleneck she wore made her pale face look even more pallid. She had overly tweezed her eyebrows and they were now colored on with a dark pencil matching the color of her long eyelashes. Khari cringed.

"This show requires elegance, grace, and beauty. Your looks will pass for beauty, but how is your grace?"

Launa's regal voice and the way she peered down at Khari made her feel small and unintelligent. Khari knew she was not blessed with any sort of poise, but she fought for confidence, lifted her chin slightly and gave Launa a sassy smile.

"Like a swan."

Khari did not have the faintest idea if she could pull off grace, but she had no intention of letting Launa know that.

"Confidence. I like confidence. Well, we will see. Jacques!"

Jacques jumped like a soldier at attention waiting for orders.

"Please review with…." She stared at Khari as if it would help reveal her name. It must have worked. "Khari…the proper way to glide down a catwalk and I do mean glide. And for heavens sake, escort her away from the view of people!" She retreated back into the tent waving Cecile and the others to follow her, leaving Jacques behind. Khari wondered if Launa really had need of them, or if she just felt better with someone at her side to order around.

A collective sigh of relief escaped them both when Launa disappeared.

"Ooooh Khari! What are you doing to me?" Jacques said in a stern whisper as he turned her around to check every angle of her dress for any unexpected flaws. Khari felt sorry for almost getting him in trouble; after all, he had always been kind to her. She was glad he had not asked her why she had left the tent. She didn't want to have to try to explain when she didn't understand the reason.

"Sorry Jacques. I'm not sure what I was thinking."

"It's all over now. However, let us get back into the tent before she returns and guillotines us," Jacques grumbled as he escorted her into the tent, lifting the bottom of the dress up and away from her feet.

Khari felt like she had endured a wild park ride after dealing with Cecile and Jacques, the unusual feelings she had with the bee, and then Launa finding her. She wasn't sure she could give anymore at that moment and surrendered to his coaxing to move quickly while trying to keep her dress from touching the ground.

As show time neared, music played soft and rhythmic, but with an edge. Launa's clothing was the last to be revealed, so Khari waited along side the other models. Some offered Khari advice and good lucks while the majority looked on, trying to keep to themselves. Launa nodded to Jacques as they passed Khari and the other girls with one last inspection.

I can't quit now, thought Khari.

The music altered to an upbeat sophisticated number marking the change of clothing lines. The rhythm of the song matched the thumping of Khari's anxious heart. Her stomach started to cramp; vomiting was a definite possibility. No more dreaming, this was real. She began to play "what if" scenarios in her mind like falling off the side of the runway, landing in a mess of dress or the form fitting dress splitting at the seams as she turned. She made an effort to renounce the nervous thoughts that were making her feel worse.

Deep breaths, she told herself.

As the man from alterations shortened the dress, she reviewed the instruction Jacques had given her—shoulders back, toes forward, neck long, butt tight, stomach in, focus straight ahead, walk on feet, ball to heel. They had rehearsed it several times in an empty corner of the tent and Khari was amazed, and delightfully amused, at the perfect poise Jacques possessed as he demonstrated the walk.

Attempting to hold still as the bottom of the dress was finished being altered, Khari closed her eyes and envisioned herself gliding as she had seen others do so many times, hoping that visualizing it would translate through her on the runway. She felt like she had it down, but that was just practice. The real thing was something completely different.

All finished, she neared the stairs that led to the runway. She noticed that the glass covering its outside walls was reflective enough that one model was using it as a mirror. The model arranged her blonde hair and inspected her almost non-existent backside before sauntering off. Khari looked around, making sure nobody was watching and rushed over to peer into the glass. The exquisite dress fell to her feet like a waterfall and the empire waist made her look like royalty. Her face shape and dark hair flowed in harmony and Khari hardly recognized herself. She thought she looked gorgeous and felt a bit sheepish at the thought. She turned around, grinning and checking every angle, unable to remove her gaze. Gratification infused within her and instead of wanting to hide, she couldn't wait to be seen, especially by Simon.

Khari heard Jacques' worried voice from the top of the stairs.

"Khari, it's your turn," he said anxiously through his clenched teeth, while attempting to reel her in with his wild hand gestures. He had already seen the other models onto the catwalk and they now streamed down the opposite stairs chatting and giggling as they went.

With renewed confidence, Khari's jitters dissipated and she felt ready to take on the catwalk. She climbed the stairs quickly, passed the last girl leaving the stage, and lifting her body in poise, entered the waiting runway.

Chapter Three ✥

Khari could not diminish the delight that filled her exuberant heart. She mingled amongst the best dressers in the world—the most beautiful, the elite, the crème de la crème of the fashion world—and they looked her way and barraged her with compliments, accompanied with cheek kisses, smiles and considerate words. On the runway, the elegant dress fed Khari's confidence and she found her footing. It was sure, steady and surprisingly natural, and she didn't just glide down the catwalk, she floated. Her steps synchronized with the music, while her shoulders connected in harmony with her perfectly swaying arms. The sun caught her at just the right moment, a personal spotlight playing off her soft features, while the breeze serenaded the airy dress against her skin. It was one of those serendipitous moments that one dreams about and now, several minutes after the runway, the same ravishing light continued to emanate from her. It was difficult to believe she felt this alluring on a day that began with her wrestling a garbage can.

Khari was beaming. Her teeth gripped her bottom lip while lovely thoughts of what she had just accomplished passed through her mind. She wanted to discuss it with every person around, but wished most of all for her mother who would have proudly run to her side. The moment held a noticeable void.

While Khari enjoyed all the attention, Simon emerged from the crowd and stole her politely from a complimenting group that had met her among the tables. He carried two slender bottles of sparkling water accompanied by lemon wedges and a gratified smile. Khari delighted in seeing his proud longing eyes and could hardly wait for his flattery. Grinning at her, he handed Khari a bottle of the bubbly water and, lifting her other hand, gently kissed her knuckles.

"I'm pretty sure when I picked you up this morning you did not mention that you would be gracing the runway in that phenomenal dress. Or did I just miss that?"

Lowering his voice he met her eyes. "You. Were. Amazing," he said, pronouncing every word as if each was equally important.

"I'm sure you knew before I came out, nothing goes on around here without Simon knowing," Khari teased. She took a drink that soothed her parched throat, grateful for its freshness.

"There were a few birds that whispered the

unbelievable news, so I did know *something* beforehand, though I was not expecting to see you so incredibly ravishing."

He leaned in and gave her a kiss that lingered long, taking Khari by surprise. She gently pushed him back.

"You know we're not alone right? There are people looking at us," Khari whispered.

"Let them look. I want them to know I am with the most beautiful girl at the party."

Just as Simon leaned in again, Jacques appeared, taking her hand while rambling a mix of French and English. Now she was positive that he was crying.

"Khari, c'est magnifique! You were a fleur blooming in the hot sand, a godsend; une triomphe!"

He reached his hands in the air in worship and then hastily pulled her into himself. He squeezed tight and Khari thought she was going to explode. Finally, he let go and rattled on without pausing for breath.

"Launa sent me over here. Of course her devilish pride would not come ask you herself, however, she knows you are set to leave for home tomorrow, but would like you to please stay and work on her team and model as well. Many people continue to ask Launa about the dress you are wearing and who the new face on catwalk was and this kind of attention does not go unnoticed from Launa. Of course she does not want anyone else to have the prize and there was already talk of an offer for you at another firm when they found out you are an artist and now model." He poked Khari in the side with his elbow and gave her a sly look.

Khari thought that her art skills had gone largely unnoticed as she merely assisted during sketch sessions. She was surprised anyone cared. Jacques was even more difficult to understand when he spoke in an exuberant voice. His high-pitched whine overtook the clarity of his words. Khari gazed at Simon for confirmation that she had understood. From the shocked smile on Simon's face she could tell she had heard correctly.

Jacques turned and looked behind him, making sure nobody was listening. "Launa never likes to feel as if someone has done her a favor, so she has demanded that you keep the dress as payment, whether you come to work for her or not. It is yours, mon cheri."

Khari was speechless. This was her ticket to stay. It happened at the last possible moment, but she didn't care. Of course she wanted to take the offer. In disbelief at the unexpected news of an incredible job and a one of a kind dress, Khari passed from one thought to the next contemplating her options and the ramifications of each one. A life-altering proposal was just placed in her lap like a heavy bowling ball. Working for Launa would be high stress, but the recognition would be incredible. Having amazing days like this one, again and again, appealed greatly to Khari and she was sure she never wanted to leave.

"Mon Cheri, do not agree now. She wants an answer within the week. Here is her card."

Jacques gave her Launa's business card, white with a black-sketched pattern across the front. Her name was large and elegant and centered perfectly above her phone number and office address. Khari, unsure of how to show her gratitude, put out her hand to shake his.

"Thanks for everything. I'll let her know as soon as I figure out what I'm going to do."

"No. Thank *you*. Today you saved my standing with Launa and possibly my job." He kissed her cheeks and turned away.

"Now you have no excuse not to stay with me," Simon said in his suave manner while stretching his arm around her.

She was at a loss for words. She could not help feeling elated at the excitement of the opportunities before her. It began to swell within her like a sponge immersed in water.

After Simon changed into a tuxedo, it was a short taxi ride to the upscale after party held in the famous National Art Gallery. Khari had always dreamed of visiting such an art museum before she came to London, but, in the moment, she was simply pleased her dress suited the venue. She wanted to wear it as long as possible and continue to revel in the gratification it granted.

After several dances and a great deal of chatter with the sophisticated crowd, Khari began to relax beside Simon at one of the tables that lined the dance floor. The table was dimly lit, creating a delicate ambiance to the evening. They chatted with ease in between bites of food, yet Khari's spirit waned and she found herself listening apathetically; fading in and out of conversation as the night drew on. In the slowing moments of a hectic day, Khari began to relive the morning occurrence with the bee and the experience with the dead one she had found later. There was an undeniable presence stirring each time she encountered them. Or perhaps, it had been nothing more than stress.

The chatter and clanging tableware around her began to grow louder and Simon's voice slowly faded into the distance. The excitement of the fashion show lifted and she now felt weighed down by its erratic occurrences and the fact that it was now ending. She thought about both the job offer and her mother who would have loved to have been there to see it all happen. It seemed difficult to imagine not having her mother around permanently. Being away for one year was one thing, but making an entire life so far away began to frighten Khari. Besides being with her mother, she didn't want to have anything to do with the life she had in Oregon. She had started a new life here and was not looking forward to returning or to seeing people back home, one person in particular.

Simon picked eagerly through the fish on his plate, placing tiny bites into his mouth as he mumbled simultaneously to Khari.

"What a great day for you, Khari. Do you realize what happened? Fate has taken you into its arms and kissed you! It would make me so happy to have you stay here." Placing his fork on his plate, he finished chewing and wiped his mouth with a cloth napkin while gazing into her face with his light blue eyes. His hair was still as perfectly placed as it had been at the start of the day. Khari loved the attention she was receiving, but it was slightly unnerving coming from Simon who normally seemed only half there as his mind was focused mainly on work.

"I would love to stay. Except, for being away from my mother. I've been away for so long already." Khari's voice faded. "It's been difficult to be so far from her." She hesitated slightly at the sound of her words, unsure of how he would react to such a personal confession. She was sure his face looked disappointed.

He paused, pulled his white cuff down and straightened it. With a brisk cleaning sweep of his fingers across his dark jacket, he responded deprecatingly, "Of course. But aren't you past the point of needing your mother by your side?"

Khari was surprised at his curt response and felt defensive.

"Well, I thought because you are always with your parents you would understand."

"Being with my parents is different. It's business. We are respectful towards one another and we help each other out if needed. I never bother them with my personal affairs or vice versa. They raised me already. I don't need them to take care of me anymore."

Khari straightened in her red velvet seat.

"I'm not eight years old, if that's what you're implying. I'm not looking to have my nose wiped. My mother is my best friend." Khari could feel her face turning red and hoped he noticed as she stared him in the eyes.

He looked somewhat shocked at her response. He took her hand in an attempt to smooth things over. "I didn't realize you were so passionate about your mother. That's fine if you want her here, just be sure it doesn't get in the way of your future. You have had a one of a kind opportunity just handed to you, and you'd be foolish to throw it away."

He kissed her hand before releasing it and returned to his meal. She tried to forget about his cold comments, but was finding it difficult. She studied him as he continued to eat his fish in proportionately small bites, habitually sipping water after each one. She wondered if she loved him. Her mind wandered to the night he kissed her for the first time, only a few months after he had befriended her. He walked her home from the tube station. They talked and laughed all the way to her place and as she neared the door lock with her keys, Simon artfully snatched her waist with both hands and simply stared at her for a time. Khari, surprised at his touch, didn't know where to place her arms and they found themselves awkwardly bent in the air seeking a proper landing spot. She finally rested them around his neck, keys still in hand, and peered at him quizzically.

"May I kiss you?" he whispered, leaning into her face in a presumptuous manner, even before he had finished his bold question. Khari was unsure if he assumed she would say *yes,* or simply didn't want to hear *no,* but without time to respond, she reluctantly accepted his moist lips. It wasn't that she wasn't attracted to him, after all his exterior was so perfect it was as if he was chiseled from a rock and polished, left gleaming for the world to admire. Yet, it was this perfection that was unnerving to be around as she second-guessed herself much of the time.

The kiss lingered, but was not overdrawn. Hands touched backs, and they embraced casually. Saying nothing, he released her subtly, smiled his ravishing smile and gazed into her eyes. He finished, just as quick and unapologetic as he began, said good night and left Khari on the doorstep, incredibly confused and a little tingly from his touch. Days after, they seemed to mesh well, the awkwardness ceased and they spent an increasing amount of time together. Now, Khari wondered what feelings she really held for him. Maybe he had only been a distraction from her loneliness. She loved the exciting places and prestigious people he had introduced her to. Yet, there was something endearing about him, such as the way he fawned after her.

"Khari, are you all right? You're barely touching your crusted halibut." Simon stared at her while he rubbed her bare arm with his hand.

"Yes. Of course. I'm fine," she answered. Grinning, she took a large bite of her roll in demonstration of her satisfactory state.

The background music changed into a soft waltz as they finished up their meal. Some of Simon's friends joined them at the table and Khari tried to keep up with the conversation while secretly wishing for a good reason to be excused. Not finding one, she smiled courteously and laughed at all the right moments, even though her real thoughts were elsewhere. Losing interest, Khari gazed away casually, and noticed a tiny dot just above their heads silently floating among the chandeliers. Attempting not to make herself noticed by the others, Khari glanced up intermittently as it darted around and then paused and perched on the edge of one of the centered white lights. She inched forward in her seat to get a closer look, but it left its resting place and started toward the door in the wall farthest from where they sat.

Khari rose and left the table with a polite and unnoticed "excuse me, I'm going to find the restroom" before following the creature. Loud laughter continued behind her as she made her way across the room through the dancing couples, with her head held high in order to keep an eye on the insect. She knew it could disappear at any moment in such a spacious place and she desperately needed to find out why their presence continued to trail her. This was the third bee she had encountered today and she could not deny the strangeness of each visit, if she dared call them that. Although her memories were sketchy, she was sure she had once been connected to them. Or was it all in her dreams?

The speck of a creature slipped through a closing door behind a thin waiter carrying an oversized dinner tray. Knowing she wasn't supposed to leave the designated room, Khari paused momentarily and checked behind her for any of the white shirted ushers that might stop her from crossing into the private gallery. No one was watching, so she pushed through the door and entered the spacious hall leading to several different rooms. She lifted her dress out of the way as the door clicked tight behind her. Yellow light streamed from the room diagonally across from Khari and she could hear the sound of someone's satisfied whistles, along with the clanging of glassware as the caterers gathered the dishes. Following a mere hunch, Khari turned right into the long dark hall, still searching the ceiling for the direction of the bee. If it had gone into the catering room she couldn't follow, so she hoped it had chosen the dark path of the empty gallery.

Several paces into the darkness, Khari could hear the buzz of the bee's wings as it echoed through the stillness. Shadowy outlines rimmed each side of the hall, but in the dim light Khari could not make out the details of the paintings. Walking slightly on her toes, just enough to lift her heels from the wood floor so only a gentle tick could be heard, she followed the soft lull of the bee down the corridor and into an expansive adjoining room.

As Khari stepped inside the empty room, she realized she had entered the landscape section of the gallery. An array of different scenes came in and out of view as she passed them, flashing momentarily in the low light of the surrounding fixtures which shone softly like night lights in the vast darkness. She could just make out the bee landing gently on the wall beside a large painting, which from a distance appeared as nothing more than odd, misshapen blotches. She turned to survey her surroundings before approaching the opposite wall, ensuring no one else was around.

Nearing the bee, a black dot on the gray lit wall, Khari was struck by the majestic silence of the moment. She felt a quiet admiration for the beauty that she was a part of. She had imagined herself visiting the art one day, to savor the great talent, but never dreamed she would be sneaking around the pieces in the dark in search of a bee. She was sure it was completely ridiculous, yet here she was.

Nearly holding her breath, Khari stood in front of the motionless bee just as it skipped onto a large painting that covered almost the entire wall. The strokes of paint were thick and it made her miss the luscious feeling of dragging color across a blank canvas to create something beautiful. It was bathed in shades of green; lanky reeds and expansive trees made up the scene. Among the foliage, a small group of half-clothed people ranging from small children to elderly emerged. They were each adorned with smiles of obvious laughter and some carried baskets on their hips and others flowers in their hair. The painting seemed to echo her Native American heritage, but she still did not comprehend what it was she was looking at.

"Is this what you wanted me to see? Did you guide me here?" Khari whispered to the bee that still waited silently on the painting. It was preposterous that an insect would know who she was and try to lead her anywhere. She snickered under her breath and after a few more moments of examining the beauty of the landscape, Khari was about to return to the party.

She felt foolish following this tiny creature into the

restricted museum and risking getting caught. She decided to return to the gala, but just as she was ready to turn away, a tiny piece of red in the painting caught her eye. It was in the background, atop a jutting cliff looming just behind the group of people. She squinted, trying to make out the red smudge, and quickly realized it was a man clad in some type of red cloak, watching over the individuals in the foreground. Although insignificant in the distance, Khari felt his importance.

The moment the figure came clear, she felt the sacred power of the man and her breath left her, causing her to step back slightly, almost falling. She could feel the intensity of a land and people she felt close to, similar to those in the painting. They spoke to her heart and she sensed their whispers and gentle chants, which had fallen upon her earlier. This time they intensified and grew in strength and volume. A unified song seemed to soak into her skin, reaching deep into her soul, and all at once she remembered those tugging feelings of responsibility she had so long forgotten, mingled with a profound despair of something lost that she could never find. Why was it returning? She did not want that same feeling that had plagued her like a dark heavy cloud she was unable to escape. It was a nagging that she was supposed to do something more, but she never understood what. She only knew that whatever it was, it called to her. Frustrated and panicked, Khari backed away from the picture hoping to stop the surge from coming, but it only intensified, sending her to her knees.

"Please. I don't understand. What am I supposed to

do?" she cried out in anguish just as someone grabbed her shoulders from behind.

"Khari! What are you doing?" Simon stood before her clearly yelling as loudly as he could while still maintaining a soft whisper. He glanced intensely around to ensure they were alone.

With the overwhelming emotions still within her, Khari could hardly speak and with languid breath she stammered out an answer.

"I...I...I don't know."

"Well, what I do know is you're going to get us kicked out and embarrassed in front of the entire crowd. You must be insane. Stand up and let's get out of here." He helped her to her feet and wrapped his arms around her shoulders to help her balance. Her legs felt feeble and her head sizzled with confusion.

Khari was desperate for understanding, some type of confirmation from the solid world that what she heard and felt was not just her imagination. But this is what had separated her from others her entire life. She glanced back at the painting half searching for the bee, but couldn't find it. She was sure it had lead her to this spot and encouraged her to remember the emotions she had tried to escape. Khari could barely breathe and she feared what would happen next, but she had to tell Simon. She caught her breath as they awkwardly made their way out the door and down the dark hall.

"Simon, did you hear anything? I mean, any voices?"

"What do you mean voices?" he impatiently blurted while trying to open the heavy door marked EXIT, still searching nervously for anyone around.

"You know. People whispering." It had been so loud and clear to her. She just hoped he had heard it as well.

"Khari. You're not making any sense. I never heard anything more than you speaking incoherently to yourself."

This confirmed her fear that she was the only one who was being spoken to. Khari felt deflated. Maybe she was crazy. She was unsure of what to say next and cowered under the indignation of his tightened squeeze. They pushed through the heavy doors and found themselves at the front of the building. He let go of her and Khari now found sure footing on her own. He looked her in the eye, standing just taller than she, and glared at her. She felt like a child being scolded.

"I know you are under a great deal of pressure after what transpired today and the job offer presented to you, but you have to get a handle on yourself Khari. You wandered away from the party into restricted parts and I found you on your knees trembling and talking to yourself in a dark gallery. It was very reminiscent of how I discovered you this morning with that bee on your face. You're acting as if you're losing your mind."

Khari trembled at the words. She understood why he would think it and looked away shrinking into herself.

Simon placed his arms around her. "Come with me. Let's at least get out of here. We can sort this out later."

Numb, Khari did as Simon suggested and went with him a few paces to where the limos and taxis waited. Her insides continued to echo emptiness. In the loud hustle of the street, there was silence within her. She tried to listen for the comfort of consolation, but found none. She thought about the nagging that had haunted her for so long. She had hoped London and all of its diversions would hold the cure, but it hadn't, and now she knew there was no hiding from her dissolving self.

She began to feel queasy as she entered the cab with Simon, trying to mull over how she had become who she was, and what she was truly meant to accomplish. Simon gave the driver his address just as a group of voices came calling after them. His friends neared the black cab. "Just act normal," Simon whispered to Khari before the men entered.

The words stung Khari more than any physical slap could. Her entire being was wounded and she could no longer move. She finally realized that it was impossible for her to be normal. She had tried since she was little, but had always known that something within her was different. An unknown cloud had hovered over her and she could no longer run from it. Here she was, thousands of miles from the home that she had jumped at the chance to escape, hoping to leave behind the strangeness, and it still followed and tormented her. It was time to admit it was hopeless.

To Khari, everything slowed. She moved, but was unsure how, as a thick weight of sadness surrounded her. The others entered the taxi and her mind reeled as they chattered on. She looked out the window and felt a storm in the calm night; the storm brewed not in the sky, but in her aching heart. She turned farther into the window, away from the others. She was sure the ache from her chest was rising to tears, leaking from the crack in her spirit. One tear dropped and then another, until they flowed freely. Khari could not stop them.

In a strange daze, she heard her voice beg the driver to stop. She kissed Simon on the cheek and fled through the open door. She could hear his voice behind her like a distant cry as she walked through the moonlight, but couldn't answer. Finally, there was the sound of the taxi pulling away and then silence. As she removed the heels from her feet, she held onto a nearby pole, trying to balance against her shaking. The sobs erupted and Khari's heaving stomach forced her to stay still and let them come.

She stood on the dark street in her gorgeous dress, wishing she could tear it from her crumpled body. She felt uglier than ever before.

Chapter Four ❦

Khari woke from a sudden jolt that caused her to grip her armrests in panic. The turbulence was short lived, but the boost of adrenaline through her startled body left her completely alert and searching for a reminder of where she was. Quickly, she realized she was on her flight home. The sound of pinging glass cups and soft voices, mingled with the smell of coffee, signaled preparations for arrival.

She had only fallen asleep for a moment, but it was long enough for the fiery dream to come again. Once more she took in deep breaths and leaned back in her seat until the feelings passed. Just like the other dreams, nothing was discernable among the flames and faded black images. It still didn't make any sense.

"Heated towel or water?" a male voice asked. She opened her eyes to a flight attendant smiling down at her.

"Yes. Both please," Khari answered taking the items and placing them on the tray in front of her.

She drank her glass of water and wiped her face with the refreshing towel. Feeling cold, she tightened the thin blanket covering her bare legs and pulled a light sweater over her arms. Although the afternoon sun shone through the airplane window, it couldn't compete with the persistent air conditioning wafting overhead.

She stretched her stiff arms in front of her as she looked out into the cloud-carpeted sky, searching for signs of their current location. Below, she could barely make out lines converging into other lines, creating strange designs as if drawn in the sand. Mountains rose from the ground in different spots appearing as mere anthills. Nothing looked familiar from such a height. She looked at her watch confirming what she had suspected. They were only an hour away from landing in Seattle. It was a two-hour drive home from there.

It felt good to finally sleep a little, even with the unsettling dream, but her mind wouldn't quiet as she mulled over the past and scrutinized her guesses for the future. The nagging that had seized her heart remained and she had given up trying to shake it. Along with the unwelcome emotions, it felt strange being suspended in the air between two different worlds, one she had just left and the other she was returning to, not really part of either one. She thought about both of them, each feared and loved for different reasons. Her thoughts drifted mostly to London.

Simon never found Khari. She refused to open the

door the first and second time he came pounding, begging her to come out. She knew that if she tried to explain, he wouldn't understand. They didn't think the same. Hiding herself away, she packed her bags hoping to make sense of herself. She considered everything, trying to find peace, over again and again, but there was none to be had.

She could feel the tugs and pulls growing within her. Instead of trying to run anymore, she had to find out what they meant. With her last item packed, she wrote a letter to Launa explaining that she would not be returning, stamped it, and left it for the postman. With that, she slipped away to the airport, unseen by any familiar soul; Launa's dress left hanging in the closet.

She hoped she would never have to divulge the details of the previous day to anyone, except possibly her mother. Would her mother think her as strange as Simon did? She wouldn't think so, but at this point she was seriously questioning her sanity. Her mother had never made her feel crazy and shone with tolerance and unconditional acceptance in situations where Khari gritted her teeth with annoyance. She was able to not only point out the good in Khari, but the good in all people and urged Khari to do the same. "We all have faults," her mother would tell her. "If we stayed away from everyone who possessed them, we would be awfully lonely." When the moment was right, Khari would try to discuss what was going on. If she could trust anyone, it was her mother.

After an announcement from the cockpit, everyone

prepared for landing. Khari snuck into the bathroom to freshen up and gathered her magazines and mostly blank sketchbook into her purse. She had tried desperately to draw anything she looked at, but the overwhelming emotions she had been feeling had overwhelmed her and she ended up with nothing but a blank page. She just couldn't concentrate. She wasn't sure she would be able to draw or paint ever again, the joy of it had somehow left her.

Khari ran her hands over her red dress that had rumpled from the long sit and smoothed her hair softly behind her ears. She wished there was a way to remove the nervous ripples that coursed through her body. The plane descended enough that out Khari's window the sparse trees began melting together into large forests and lines were now recognizable roads. Trees gave up their space in areas where houses and shopping centers emerged. Tiny ants and their raised homes were again speeding cars and mountains. Khari could see the ocean a ways off and boats moving toward and away from the shore. She felt her insides turn at the common scene and took deep breaths as the plane's wheels squealed down from their hiding places. Khari gripped the edge of her seat and closed her eyes as the gliding plane connected with the ground and crept to a rest.

Khari's turn to deplane came quickly, and she began to push her way down the aisle. A bold lettered newspaper article lying across a now abandoned seat caught her eye. The headline read, "Number of Dying Bees is on the Rise." Khari let out an audible gasp that seemed to echo through the nearly empty plane. She didn't notice the multiple eyes turning her way as she tugged at her lip with thumb and finger and hunkered over the seat to read the paper. She skipped all the extra stuff and went straight for the bold highlights in the side columns that read, "Scientists around the world work together to find the cause of bee deaths," and "Professor Swartzhouser in Miami, Florida, United States, claims that the bee population is dwindling because the bees themselves are not staying together. The bees in the colonies are dispersing, possibly leaving the hives without proper warmth or nutrition. Why they are leaving has yet to be determined."

"Excuse me, ma'am, we're deplaning the aircraft. May I help you find your luggage?" One of the flight attendants hung over Khari giving her a friendly smile that harmonized with the genteel blue handkerchief tied around her long neck.

"Oh, no, sorry. I wasn't paying attention. I have my stuff, thanks." Khari lifted herself up and threw her bag over her shoulder.

"Would you like to keep your newspaper?"

"No, I'm finished." Khari attempted a smile.

She fumbled her way off the plane thinking of the bees, trying to remember what she swore she knew, but had somehow forgotten. It was frustrating to feel as if revelation was right before her, but she couldn't place what it was or where it had come from. It was like her heart and her mind were working against one another.

In the airport, overhead announcements and bright

lights distracted her frustrated thoughts and awakened her senses from sleep. She felt she was emerging into a new world. It was odd to hear American accents after listening to the constant barrage of British inflections for so long. Khari smiled at the familiarity that had been lost for a time.

After finding the rest of her luggage, she made her way to the exit and out the door. A smell of salt hiding in the air's warm thickness seeped around her and clung to her like moss to a stone. She could tell a quick rain had passed through from the damp sidewalks and rain spattered windshields of cars passing by. Through the crowding of people, Khari searched for her mother's blue pickup. She spotted it easily. Her mother stood on her tiptoes at its side, in an attempt to see over the passing heads of people. Khari smiled. She could not help the rush of elation from the sight of her sweet mother and though just steps away, she felt too far. She struggled quickly toward her mother while attempting to balance two shoulder bags and rolling a suitcase.

"Mom!" Khari called out as she awkwardly ran to her side.

Her mother turned in recognition of Khari's voice and bounced with delight into her arms. Rapture chased away nervous jitters and they enfolded into one another, simultaneously squealing, jabbering and crying. No more weekly letters and occasional phone calls. Khari had her in her arms.

"My beautiful little Kharishma returned a woman. Look at you. I thought you were finished growing!" Khari was surprised at hearing her full name again. A name filled with meaning, it invoked the somber image of the night Khari was born. Khari was always amazed the way her mother told of that night, with love and joy despite the pain and fear. Now, her mother was the only one who used her full name. Khari had never cared for it and had shortened it long ago. She felt silly as a Native American to have such a foreign name. Now, coming from her mother, it was like hearing sweet music.

"You cut your long hair!" Khari said, pulling gently at the ends of her mother's shoulder length hairstyle. Since the day Khari was born, her mother wore long black hair. Although Khari thought the cut was cute on her, it was peculiar to see it so different.

"Even I can be stylish," her mother lovingly retorted. The light streaks in her mother's brown eyes accented her natural olive complexion. It was refreshing to see skin so pure without make-up; her mother lovelier than any supermodel covered in synthetics.

"And don't worry, that's probably the only change we've had around here. Everything is pretty much the same as when you left."

As they heaved the bags over the side of the truck into the back, Khari thought she noticed a hint of worry in her mother's countenance. Between smiles, her brows crinkled at the center of her forehead as if she was forcing an unwanted thought from her mind.

"I have a pot of slow cooking beans with a side of bread waiting for you. Let's go before they burn. There's so much I want to ask you." Her mother smiled and winked as she lifted herself into the truck and opened the door from the inside for Khari. Among other things on the truck, the passenger side handle never worked. When she was younger, Khari loved to slide in and out the window. She felt fearless passing through at such a height.

"I can't believe this truck still runs. You must wash it with water from the fountain of youth."

"It will never go. If it were going to die, it would have done it a long time ago. Trusty Rusty." She patted the dashboard lovingly as they both giggled and pulled away from the chaotic airport and onto the highway. Conversation flowed easily between them and Khari sank back into the comfort of her mother's presence, as one would a large comfortable sofa. Khari gave the latest details of her life—the runway, the dress, the job offer—and her mother hung on every word, smiling proudly and demanding specifics.

"So, are you going to take the job? Do you have the dress?"

Khari lamented that she didn't have the dress to show her. She wished for a moment she had not left it behind.

"I can't...sorry...I left it in London." For some reason there was awkwardness at the idea of telling her mother any more. She didn't want to startle her with the strange occurrences so soon.

"But didn't they give it to you?" her mother inquired gently, eyes half on the road, half on Khari.

Khari fidgeted with items in the compartment in front of her, picked up a road map and pretended to study it. She steadied her voice.

"Well...yes...but I just couldn't keep it. It's hard to explain. I already answered no to the job. I just can't imagine working for that woman." Khari tried to laugh, but ended up sounding like she was choking.

She felt her mother stare at her for a moment, probably sensing that there was something deeper Khari wasn't telling her.

"I thought you might bring Simon home with you. Will he be coming to visit?"

Here goes another red flag, Khari thought.

"Well...no. I decided long distance relationships never work out."

Khari tried to act calm, but the more effort she put into it, the more frazzled she became. She attempted to fold the map correctly several times before her frustration escalated and she crumpled it to the floor.

"Sorry," Khari half whispered as she stared out the window, feeling the fierce emotions rise within her. Her mother's hand brushed the side of Khari's head, softly stroking her hair.

"Do you want to talk about it?"

"Not yet if that's all right."

"Of course," her mother said quietly. She was silent after that and Khari wondered if she was terribly disappointed in her.

"Mom? We've been talking about me the whole time. How are you doing? How's the business?"

"Great. Virginia and I couldn't keep up with the clients and events so we hired a new girl last week. She's a great server and very organized, which helps tremendously. Just in time, too. We have an event in a city a long drive from home in just a few days. I hate to leave you so soon. You're welcome to come with us. I would never turn down an extra hand." She smiled and patted Khari's knee affectionately.

Khari's mother owned a small catering company. Unlike other companies in the area, her mother served home style cooking which was a hit. When she was younger and couldn't be left alone, Khari had to accompany her mother or stay with her uncle. Although Khari disliked cooking as much as a burn on her skin, she always chose to go. She loved her uncle, but nothing was worse than staying at his house for a whole night listening to endless details about his boomerang collection. Khari's desire to always go along is why her mother chose to homeschool Khari and why she had graduated earlier than others her age.

"I wouldn't mind going," Khari answered.

"Great! It will be fun to have you with us." Khari's mother seemed not only ecstatic that she was coming, but strangely relieved.

Time passed quickly, and stores and gas stations appeared less frequently on their drive as the conversation slowed. Khari tried to close her eyes while her mother seemed lost in heavy thought. Green mileage signs were the only indicators of their location and, with only forty minutes left, Khari began to feel excitement well up at the thought of once again being a part of the land she loved. She tried to embrace that excitement and forget the nervousness clawing at her stomach.

Khari's mom quieted the scratchy radio and glanced at Khari. "There's something I wanted to talk to you about before we arrived home," she said. Khari peered at her mother. She could once again see the worried look on her mother's brow.

"A couple of nights ago, the house was broken into while I was catering an event. Luckily, I wasn't home. But I want you to be careful around the house if I'm not there. I don't think we should worry too much, just be aware."

"What did they take?" Khari asked, sitting up from the comfortable position she had taken on the vinyl seat.

"That's what I can't figure out. Nothing's missing. A back window was broken in the kitchen so they could get in, but once they entered, they didn't take anything. The house was in shambles, as if they were looking for something specific, but the cash in my drawer was still there along with my jewelry. It's had me completely baffled."

Khari was horrified at the thought of someone pillaging through their things. The idea that they wanted something more than money sent an uncomfortable chill through her. "Did you call someone?"

"Yes. I was frightened they were still in the house so I hurried out and drove to the neighbors. Turns out, nobody was hanging around, just a big mess. Uncle Louis and others came to help clean up and Sam offered to install a new window."

Khari's mom hesitated at Sam's name. To Khari, hearing his name was like a slap to the face. Her mom must have seen the disturbance in her because she looked at her for a moment and waited.

"Sam? Does he still come around?" Khari asked quietly. She fiddled with her fingers resting in her lap and tried to steady her voice.

"He comes around once in a while to check on things. He tries to help me out around the house."

Sam ranched with his uncle, but he seemed to know how to do a little bit of everything, even cook, so he was always sought around town to do odd jobs. Khari's heart raced along with her mind. *Had he asked about her? Was he dating someone? What was he doing now?* Asking any of them was unthinkable.

"Are you going to be all right seeing him again? I know you haven't spoken since you left. I want to make sure it won't be too hard for you."

Her mother didn't have an inkling of the difficulties she was already faced with. Khari forced a smile. 'I'm sure I'll be fine. It might be strange to see him, but I've moved on." Khari hoped she was telling the truth.

The sullied air was far behind them and the sweet pure breezes began pouring through the open windows, as if welcoming Khari home. She rested her arm on the outside of her door, reveling the feel of the fresh current against her skin as she breathed in deep. Turning off the highway, the trees began to pull away from the road some and separate until they gave way just enough that Khari could see her small town of Blue Ridge in the distance.

The surrounding valley was green with occasional lakes and rivers through it. Scattered throughout the valley was the small town and its skirt of farmland laid quietly underfoot a looming mountain peak that stood guard over the small population.

The sight of her town evoked a leap of joy within her and, for a moment, the tidal wave of nerves dissipated and she was left with only the wind in her face, the tingle of sun against her skin, and the smell of spring blossoms penetrating her nostrils. With her eyes closed, she could feel the damp soft earth and hear the whistle of the wind when it blew through the tall grass just so. Somehow, she could hear the buzzing of bees wings, the silky feel of butterfly's wings and the tickle of the beetles against her skin. Ancient trees surrounded her, sharing with her their majesty. She drowned in the feeling of bliss as if she had lost herself in thick mud. But the delightful emotions began to fade as dark clouds gathered in her mind and choked out any goodness. Hot flames rose around her chasing away the insects and consuming the mighty trees. Its heat surrounded her. She tried to find a way out, but was called back by hundreds of voices begging for her help. Khari cried out in anguish just as her mother's voice and the creaking of an opening door pulled her from the scene.

"Khari. Wake up." Her mother patted Khari's shoulder.

Khari raised her slumped head and tried to place where she was. She was surprised to see they were parked in the center of town. Her mom entered the car with a bag of groceries.

"Hey. I didn't want to wake you, but you were mumbling pretty loud." Her mother glanced at her as she started the car and started off toward home. "I left you sleeping for just a second. I had to grab a couple of things. Are you okay?"

"Sorry, Mom. Just a dream," Khari apologized. She would never get used to the horrible dreams, they still made her feel crazy. She breathed in deep and brushed her hair from her face as they made their way from the city center.

Their house was more than a mile off the main road and surrounded by the neighboring expanse of trees and wildlife. Once the paved road was behind them and they had disappeared into a green wall of foliage, they turned into an unfinished access road half hidden by the bordering trees. It was extremely narrow, just wide enough for one car to pull through, and her mother's large truck often surrendered itself to the scratching of branches against its sides. At night, anyone traversing the lane was at the mercy of the road to guide them, as nothing could be seen on either side through the dense vegetation. It was one of Khari's favorite spots because of its cooler air and accompanying delicious scents, which overwhelmed the area and seemed to dampen the skin with their perfume. Khari imagined giant blossoms concealed somewhere in the green mass. She inhaled deeply, the smell of fresh trees exuding crisp life. Farther on, a dip in the road carried them down through a small but steady rill of water, which trickled its way from a nearby river. After a slight drop in the road and a sharp curve at its end, her home could finally be seen.

Chapter Five

Khari felt guilty for not helping her mother finish up the food for the upcoming catering event and the bustle from the kitchen intensified the sentiment. Still, Khari couldn't bring herself to join her. She felt uneasy around anyone since returning home a few days earlier. She felt awkward trying to make small talk when something so heavy weighed within her. Luckily, the garden had begun to wilt and weep for care and gave her something to do alone during the day. She felt a calm with her hands pushed deep in the cool earth.

Khari's mind jumped between the unpleasant end with Simon and her lost chance at an amazing life spent in exquisite London, to the suspense of seeing Sam which gnawed tirelessly at her. He had yet to bring the new window to replace the one that had been shattered during the break-in and luckily, even with different errands to town and visits to neighbors, their paths had not crossed. However, she was aware that in the small town, it was just a matter of time before they ran into one another.

Now, dressed in jeans and a t-shirt, Khari turned over on her bed and gazed at the worn picture of her mother holding her as a baby. It was Khari's favorite photo. She tried to focus on the details of the story she had heard so many times before and imagined her mother lying large with child in the middle of a lightning storm, alone and miles away from her friends and family. After the death of Khari's father, her mother had run away from their incessant voices assuring her she would be okay, voices that stung her with what she thought were lies. She lay in the cabin where she and Khari's father had once dreamed of bringing their children and grand-children, a place that she was practically raised in. She was isolated, sorting out her life, trying to figure out how she would live without him and the tossing of Khari in her womb gave her no comfort.

She expected to deliver Khari in two months and when the fluid and blood dripped from her, she knew something she wasn't prepared for was about to happen, alone in the cabin in the middle of the forest. She stayed still in the bedroom, oil lamp flickering, wishing she could stop what was about to occur. But, when the fluid ceased, the cramping began passing through her in consistent waves until, between flashes of lightning, Khari was born.

Most likely it was being thrust into the world early that took Khari's breath away, leaving her in her mother's arms, lifeless. Khari's mother felt frightened at the dead child before her. She had never been around the birth of a baby, but her inexperience allowed for her faith and hope to take over. All she could think of were the words of a song sung to her by her father when she felt sick. She sang it flawlessly, as if she had sung it every day of her life. The words and melody were as natural a sound as her heart beating and they brought a clear vision and a surety of what to do next. She massaged Khari's chest, sure she would breathe again, and, when she did, she named her Kharishma, a name from a favorite story meaning miracle.

Khari loved the amazing account and wondered how her mother could feel so many emotions twisted simultaneously together. She wished that she could be as brave and selfless, but felt like she always fell far from it.

Deciding to forget herself for the sake of her mother, Khari left her room and made her way to the lively kitchen. A sweet aroma of deep spices and nuts along with the strength of garlic and peppers filled the space. Khari's mother was famous not only for her amazing ability to cook, but also for her flawless service at catered events. She was proud of her work and it was manifested in the results. Khari found a glass in the cupboard and began filling it with cool water from the tap without anyone noticing her.

Virginia, her mother's long-time assistant, was whipping some sort of thickened sauce at the large dark wood table in the center of the room, while her mother was at the stove attentively stirring stew over a low flame. The washing machine churned beyond the kitchen and the faint sound of music played from the small radio resting in the windowsill under the taped up window, still gaping from the earlier break in. It served as a reminder that Sam would at some point be coming to fix it.

"Well, look who's here," Virginia called out in an exuberant manner.

Virginia, who was naturally blonde and sassy, reminded Khari of vanilla ice cream topped with fiery cinnamon sprinkles. She abruptly left her whipping and advanced toward Khari, arms wide in her direction. Virginia had been working with Khari's mother as her assistant for five years now. She was a fabulous cook and physically fit. Her passion was competing in marathons and triathlons. Anything that even resembled a competition, she was there. Her difficulty in life was being dismally single.

"Khari! I am so excited to see you, Darlin! Look at you! You're as gorgeous as a black skinned rabbit."

Khari wondered if that was a good thing.

"Hello, Virginia."

Khari gave her a side hug and tried not to drop the glass of water she was holding.

"We never thought the year would pass and you would be gracing us with your sweet self again," Virginia went on.

Her thick Texan accent made it obvious she was not from Oregon. She was always smiling in spite of her constant complaints about being forty and unwed.

"It's good to see you too," Khari responded as cheerfully as she could muster. "You look good. Any competitions coming up?" She thought inquiring about competition was the safe way to dodge any details about Virginia's love life.

"Competing is great. Ya know, it keeps me busy in all my free time alone. I love competing," she answered unconvincingly as she returned to whipping her sauce. "Your mother has been keeping me updated while you were away." As if she had flipped a switch her voice lowered to a faint whisper as she nudged Khari in the ribs with her pointy elbow. "Sorry about the British fella." She ended her statement with a slight wink and then sighed for a moment. "I can't understand why my love life can't find itself attached to another's. Ya know? I mean, I meet the most men out of anyone in this town travelin' around as a caterer, but still nothin. Did you hear about Lizzy Growle?" Khari didn't have time to respond to the question before Virginia continued. "She met someone in the grocery store from out of town and is getting married in a few months. Does that seem fair to you? I don't even think she *wanted* to wrestle herself a husband."

Khari was amazed at the way Virginia could vehemently complain in such a charming tone. She tried to think of something to stop her, but was drawing a blank. Luckily, her mother removed her stew from the heat and began pouring it into ceramic containers, interrupting Virginia's complaining. Khari never knew how to comfort her.

"We leave in the morning, Khari. Are you still coming?" her mother questioned glancing up at Khari momentarily from the bowls she was filling. She knew the trip would last five days with much of it driving together in the car and that questions would arise concerning herself. She didn't want to deal with such conversation, but was unsure how to get out of it. She didn't want to sound as pathetic as she felt.

The sound of rocks popping under tires in the driveway, followed by a long drawn out honking of a car horn, removed the need to respond as everyone's attention turned to the interruption.

"Looks like Uncle Louis is here. He's back from his convention and wanted to see you." Khari's mother gave her a gentle smile before pushing aside the steaming containers and reaching for a mound of pale dough that she began smoothing out across the floured table.

Louis was her only other family member besides her mother, and had taken on the role as her father. She loved him and most of the time appreciated his company, except for his obsessive collection of boomerangs.

"Why don't you go out and see him? He's been waiting to show you his new car."

"When did he get that?" Khari asked as she leaned on the windowsill and watched him step confidently from the sleek red car in dark leather boots, flannel shirt and light blue jeans. His long raven hair tied into two tight braids cascaded down the front of his shoulders with a red and orange patterned band tied tightly around his forehead. She never could figure out why he wore his hair in the Native American style. She never heard him or her mother breathe a word about their people, or demonstrate any interest in living their traditions. She stepped out of the house to meet him.

"Hello Louis!" Khari called as she walked toward him.

"Well, there's my lovely niece," he said affectionately while taking swift giant steps towards her. "Let me look at you." Louis held her shoulders and stared at her as if he was holding up a shirt in an attempt to decide if he should buy it. The deep lines across his face were more prevalent than when she had last seen him. His burly body hovered over her like a giant bear ready to maul. His dark brown eyes were almost hidden in the folds of skin around them. He shifted a toothpick from one side of his mouth to the other with only his lips. Whether plain or cinnamon flavored, he was never seen without one in his mouth.

"I can't believe my eyes. Khari is officially a lady. Look at how lovely she's grown." He spoke as if someone were in the vicinity to hear his flattery.

Khari smiled her best smile and tolerated his space invading.

"Hello Uncle Louis how are..." Before she could finish her sentence, he squeezed her head into his broad chest.

"Oh, how I missed my little girl."

Khari eased her way out of his arms as politely as possible and stood back using her folded arms like a barricade between them. He had called her that ever since she could remember.

"You know I'm nineteen now, right Uncle? You don't have to call me that anymore." Khari smiled gently at him.

"Oh. Don't mind me. I'm just amazed at how you've grown and wish you were still the little girl who loved to be carried around on my shoulder."

He walked over to the driver's side door and waved Khari in to sit down on the front seat.

"Go ahead, check it out. It's a classic. A 1960 Cadillac Eldorado." Louis removed a handkerchief and rubbed off a spot on the window. "Go on, get in. The seats are like sitting on giant pillows."

Khari couldn't care less about his shiny new car, but she attempted a grin and slid into the white leather seat just as he closed the door behind her. He crouched down so he could lean on it. The seats really did feel like pillows. He pushed a round knob next to the giant white wheel and the black top disconnected from the body of the cherry red car and rolled back into itself.

"Now this is the best way to take in the beauty of Oregon. Cruise through the mountains or green country with no restrictions. Not as good as our grandfather's connection to the land, but close wouldn't you say?" He gave Khari a light slap at the top of her shoulder. That was the first time Khari had ever heard him mention ancestors. She wanted to ask more questions, but decided against it.

"Comfy, isn't it?" he asked, still leaning on the door beside her.

"Sure. It's really nice." She patted the large white steering wheel in front of her as a gesture of sincerity.

In an attempt to end the awkward staring and

nodding of heads, Khari asked the only question that came to mind and regretted it the moment it left her mouth.

"So, how was your boomerang convention?" She opened the door and got out, shutting it behind her.

His face changed showing obvious excitement.

"Oh! Fantastic. There were boomerangs from all around the world. Most of them I had never seen before." He began speaking with intensity and using his hands a lot. "I bought one from a man who had spent time with the Australian Aborigines and had learned how to make their special boomerangs that were used in battle and hunting. It doesn't return to you like the fun ones because of its straighter shape, but it could actually be used to kill. I haven't thrown it yet. It's too perfect. Come by the house and see it."

He had over a hundred boomerangs ranging in sizes and materials. Khari had seen them a dozen times and dreaded the invitation. All she could manage was a nod in response.

"So your mom says that you have a boyfriend living over in England. What was his name?" He closed his eyes and struggled for the answer.

"Simon," Khari responded. She felt ill at the thought of having this conversation with him.

"Oh, yeah. Simon. Everyone thought you would end up with Sam. You two were inseparable since you were fifteen. It was so cute. Well, I guess we were wrong."

The ache in Khari's stomach intensified at hearing both Sam and Simon's names uttered in the same sentence.

"Will we at least be meeting the boy?"

Khari was unsure how to answer. She folded her tense arms.

"No. He lives miles away so..." She kicked at the rocks under her feet.

"Well, you should invite him to come."

To Khari's relief her mother came out the front door carrying Khari's green leather bag.

"Hello, Louis. How are you?" She placed one hand on his shoulder and, thankfully, he quit talking.

"I'm sorry to interrupt, but I'm short on walnuts for the dessert. Would you mind grabbing me some from the store, Khari?"

"I can take you if you want," Louis offered.

"Actually, Louis, I was hoping you could help me in the kitchen for a moment. You can take the truck, Khari. The keys are in it." Her mother gave her a sly wink and handed Khari her bag before waving Louis to follow her inside.

"It's good to have you home," Louis said waving good-bye.

"Good to see you Louis. Be back in a minute." Khari was relieved to escape the unpleasant Simon conversation and made her way to the old truck parked at the side of the house. She closed the door behind her and roared away.

Once in town, she pulled into a spot near the edge of a large grassy square at the center of town. The different stores, including a barbershop, bakery and post office, enclosed the park full of trees, grass and scattered benches throughout. There were spots closer to the grocer, but Khari wanted to walk through the plaza. All of the many trees were covered in pink and white blossoms and the scent was irresistible. She meandered for a time underneath the heavy laden branches, until she arrived at the doors of the quaint grocer.

Entering the store, with its artificial lights and cold floors, robbed her of the lovely sensations she felt seconds ago. She wanted to get out of there quickly, so she grabbed a basket and walked hurriedly and somewhat disoriented down the aisles.

Finding the baking section, Khari shuffled down to the bags of nuts lining the shelf. Realizing she had forgotten to ask the amount her mother needed, she threw several into the basket to be safe; she did not want to come back. Feeling perfectly satisfied with her decision to buy more than what was probably needed, she headed for the candy aisle. She needed something with peanut butter and chocolate and scanned the shelves for her favorite treat. Excited to find them, she grabbed two.

"Khari! How are you?"

Khari's heart jumped as she threw the bars into the basket and turned to see Sheffield, his dull red hair matching his Grocery Town apron perfectly. He stared at her with open arms, apparently waiting for her to jump into them. His excited voice scared her a little.

"I didn't know you were home already!" he squealed.

"How are you Sheffield?" Khari asked kindly as he wrapped his long skinny arms around her. Sheffield was always found in or near the grocery store since his family owned it. Khari had assumed he had left for college now that they were out of high school. Being home schooled until high school, Khari only had to take a couple of semesters of what felt like endless testing to graduate early. Sheffield was the only other student doing the same thing. Living in a small town and being in the exclusive advanced program, she and Sheffield did everything together and knew each other better than anyone at school. He wanted to be an architect and spoke of his engineering feats with fervor, desiring nothing more than to build in the largest cities of the world, so seeing him in the grocery store uniform surprised her.

"I just returned yesterday. What about you? Are you working here still?" She hoped her words didn't sound judgmental. His continued smile proved it hadn't bothered him.

"I am. I'm my dad's right hand around here. He had a heart attack months ago and couldn't run the business on his own. He didn't ask me to stay, but I decided to until he felt he could manage again. Plus, I'm dating someone pretty serious." His face blushed a little and continued. "Her name is Amy. We met at a wedding and I think she's the one." His smile got bigger as he spoke.

"Oh Sheffield that's great! I'm so happy for you." Khari really was relieved that he was happy. He was always the odd one left out of things in high school and Khari was one of the few friends he had.

"How about you? I heard you were dating someone in England. Is it serious?"

Was there anybody who didn't know about Simon?

"Well, no. He's in England... I'm here. It's too complicated to make it work."

"Oh. Sorry. Well, maybe something will still work out."

Khari nodded pursing her lips together. A voice over the loud speaker bellowed for Sheffield's help on aisle five. He excused himself just as excitedly as he had appeared.

"I hope to see you again soon. Maybe we can get together and you can meet Amy."

"Yeah. Sure." Khari waved good-bye as his pace accelerated down the aisle.

After he was gone, she hurried to the register to buy her things, grateful the stalky woman taking her money, didn't know her or Simon, and left through the exit.

Half way across the plaza, Khari pulled a candy bar from the plastic sack while she passed under the blooming trees. Realizing she needed her keys as she neared the truck, she began fumbling through her bag, working her candy bar filled hand awkwardly inside to find them. Unsuccessful at her struggle, she dropped the grocery bag to the ground to utilize both her hands in the search and began digging and shuffling for the keys amongst the various items inside.

In her desperate search, she forgot her surroundings and unexpectedly felt a hand on her arm. Khari's stomach knotted before she saw who it was. She knew. The hand was full of familiarity. One hand should feel like any other, but not Sam's. His hands were solid, consistently warm, and slightly coarse from arduous work. She turned to see him smiling with confidence at her, one hand leisurely in the front pocket of his jeans. A dark blue button-up shirt relaxed over a grey t-shirt which was tucked casually into his pants, showing his worn leather belt. She couldn't believe it was him.

She stood up, throwing the purse back over her shoulder, and tried to gather her emotions. His face was rugged yet innocent, with joy on his lips. His hair was full of soft waves, thick, dark and slightly disheveled. She could feel the wild texture without touching it. She knew it by heart. His green eyes danced a hello and left her speechless. She began trembling from the excitement and shock of seeing him and she hoped he didn't notice. She never expected to react this way.

"I heard you were back. You look good." He spoke with sincerity and stared at Khari with a kind of sad fondness. Khari was unsure if her voice would come when she tried to speak. She began slowly just in case.

"I...got here a few days ago. You look so good. How are things on the ranch?"

So good? What are you saying? Khari wanted to hide.

"Good, thanks," he chuckled. "The weather has been unusually dry which makes work a little easier." His voice trailed off slightly as he gazed at Khari, causing her to feel self-conscious. She tugged at her hair and placed it behind her ear.

"How was England?" he continued.

When he spoke there was an inkling of gall behind his sincerity. She wondered how much "Simon" information he had heard. She felt embarrassment rise and she stumbled on her answer.

"Uh. It went just as I hoped, I guess. But, I'm happy to be home. Even though I'm feeling completely wacked out being here, but I'm slowly adjusting."

Wacked out? I need to stop talking. Khari's hand found her cheek. She was feeling mortified at her clumsy speech and could feel the red rushing to her face. The more she tried to suppress it, the worse it got. She looked down hoping he couldn't tell.

"I was just in town checking on the new window for your mom. It should be here in a few days. Windows in old houses take longer because they need to be special ordered. Is the cover that I nailed up holding okay?"

"Oh. Yeah, it's great. Thanks for helping us out. It's unnerving that someone was in our house. I can't even think about it. I'm just relieved my mother was gone." Khari was always rambling around him. It was like secrets inside of her were drawn to his ears. She wanted to tell him all she thought and felt. She was shocked that the urge was still there.

"Sorry, I'm rambling."

"No, it's good to hear you ramble." He smiled. "I'm really sorry it happened." He placed his other hand in his pocket while lifting his shoulders. He looked as if he was deciding what his next move would be.

"Well, my uncle is waiting for me to help bring in the cattle." He pointed toward his truck. "It was good to see you."

"Oh, right. I have to go too." Khari pulled out the

keys from the now rummaged bag and again threw it over her shoulder. She bent over and lifted the plastic grocery bag. When she glanced up he was staring at her with a gentle smile.

"You're still eating the same candy bars." He chuckled at the treat she held in her other hand.

Khari froze and glanced at the chocolate bar, feeling somewhat like a child again.

"I guess. I haven't eaten one since I left. I was craving them." Khari smiled.

"Yeah." He ran his hand through his hair and stepped back hesitating to leave. "It was good to see you."

"You, too."

Khari was about to turn to leave when Sam suddenly stepped toward her, paused, and then eased his solid arms around her and held her tight. She sank easily into his large frame and nestled there for a moment. His earthy honeyed smell hit her and she breathed in deeper trying to drink in the scent. After a few moments, he released her slowly and gave a small wave as he backed away.

"Bye, Khari." He ran across the street, jumped up into his white truck and slowly pulled away. Khari still had not moved. She was unsure she ever could. The pain in her heart had returned.

Chapter Six

Khari couldn't sleep. Besides the continuous dreams, two days had passed since seeing Sam and she found herself sinking into quiet confusion once again. She replayed her awkward words with him repeatedly in her mind, picturing his face, his eyes, the way he had nervously held her and then left, and she wondered at the meaning behind each movement. Did he have to pull himself together when he reached the ranch, just as she tried to do when she returned home?

When Khari had arrived with the walnuts, her mother and Virginia were hard at work, laughing as they julienned and sautéed, oblivious to the sputter of the truck pulling in. They hadn't noticed Khari's quiet entrance until the plastic sack landed noisily on the table. Khari, in a solemn stupor, lifted the walnuts from the bag, making every effort not to show her sadness, yet failing as her red face was smeared in anguish. Her mother recognized her fight to steady herself and knew she had seen Sam. Quickly, Khari found herself a child again, wrapped in her mother's arms, silent tears streaming a steady path down her cheeks. So many forgotten emotions were rekindled at the sight of him. She had convinced herself that she possessed sufficient strength to live again in his vicinity, although deep inside she had known the truth.

That day, Khari's mother busied Khari with odd jobs, attempting to distract her from her brooding. From painting the swing hanging on the front porch to pruning the orchard, she kept herself occupied, fueled by the slight anger at her foolish heart. The final job of clearing and planting the largest garden hidden in the backyard took the next two days and gave her an excuse to stay home from the five-day catering trip. Her mother reluctantly left her alone and Khari spent that time hoping to rid herself of Sam's memory. But, her efforts were in vain.

Adding to Khari's depressed state was a head cold, which had intensified quickly. Khari had fought not to succumb to the illness as she worked in the garden, but as she slowly smoothed the dirt around the fresh tomato plants, her throat began to scratch. And as she turned the hose to the space, leaving pools of water covering the ground, she began to sneeze. A chill rippled through her, even though she lingered in the warm sun. She couldn't rub it away and an attempt to cover herself with a sweater didn't warm her. Quickly following the chill, a tickle entered her throat accompanying the ache that inched its way into places Khari had never felt before. Every symptom arrived in succession—aches through her body, her head filled with heat, and her nose began to run. The health she enjoyed just moments earlier was replaced by an overwhelming illness. In an instant, she felt completely awful.

Barely making it to her room, she collapsed in her bed and found herself stuck there, unable to do anything but feel dreadful and ponder her sorry state. On the phone, her mother was ready to cancel her venue and return to Khari, but Khari assured her all she needed was sleep and she would be fine. Now she wished she hadn't been so confident and longed for her mother there.

After a day of grappling with the malady inside of her, and the difficult thoughts in her mind, she lay in her fever as if in a pool of hot water and tried to think on something other than Sam. She pulled the third layer of blanket tighter over the two underneath, not feeling any difference as she once again shivered. She yanked at the wool socks on her legs wishing they could reach her knees, but soon gave up trying to lengthen them. She curled her knees into her chest and pulled her long nightshirt down until her legs were enveloped inside its softness. Her head felt as if it was filled with wet heavy sand and she tried to suppress the unforgiving cough that wouldn't quit.

She reached for another tissue and pulled a clean one from the box that lay surrounded by a sea of crumpled, damp, used ones. She just couldn't get comfortable. Khari made an attempt to lift her sore body from the mattress whose softness she couldn't feel through the ache of her muscles. Her stomach began to growl and she knew she needed to eat. She stuffed two new tissues into her nose and wrapped a purple robe loosely around herself. After adjusting her socks straight again, Khari shuffled from the room down to the kitchen. She longed for vegetable soup, not only to eat, but to let its healing steam waft gently into her puffy face.

In the kitchen, standing upright after lying down for so long increased the pressure in her head and she stumbled around the kitchen looking for an onion. There were none in the hanging wire basket where the garlic, bananas and a few apples found themselves, so she opened the pantry and stepped inside, searching the shelves with her irritated eyes. She leaned on the door, squinting at the bright light over her throbbing head.

"Finally," Khari groaned to herself at the sight of the single yellow onion sitting innocently next to a brown sack of potatoes.

After filling a large pot with water and placing it atop the stove, she ignited the flame underneath, weakly pulled a knife from its wooden holder, and began her attempt at peeling and slicing the vegetable upon the large butcher block left next to the stove. Khari leaned her stomach against the counter top, struggling to keep herself upright, and chopped the onion as quickly as her slow tired body was able. She hoped she could finish the chopping without it burning her retinas, but half way through the process the invisible moisture from the onion passed the clumped tissues in her nose and saturated her eyes. Khari closed them quickly, but the sting seemed to spread and worsen. In desperation, she dropped the knife and open-ed the door to the nearby freezer and stuffed her head inside, allowing the frigid air to hit her eyelids, which she forced open to mere cracks. Amazingly, it worked, and the sting dissipated in the cold. She stayed there for sev-eral moments enjoying the relief.

"Are you all right?"

A voice from behind startled her and she ended up wrestling the freezer door as she pulled her head back in alarm.

Standing in the doorway, dampened from the rain and with toolbox in hand, was Sam.

"Sam! What are you doing here?" Khari couldn't think of anything else to say as she tightened the robe around herself and glanced from him to the floor, unsure of which to rest her eyes on.

"I'm...so sorry. I spoke with your mother last week and she said you would both be out of town. She gave me a key to get in to fix the window." The confused look on his face told Khari he felt as embarrassed as she did, until his concerned mouth turned into a slight grin.

"Are you okay?" he asked trying not to laugh.

Khari stood there in her wool socks and robe, hair in disarray, and, *Oh no*, thought Khari. *The tissues.* Mortified, she yanked them from her nose and pushed them into her oversized robe pockets. She spoke in a nasally voice, eyes fixed on the ground.

"I guess my mother forgot to tell you that I didn't

go with them. I have this terrible cold, or flu, or whatever it is. It's awful. I just came down to make some vegetable soup and found an onion and put the water on to boil and, while I was cutting it, my eyes started to burn, and so I felt like I needed to cool them off." She paused for a moment, dreading to say it. "So I stuck my head in the freezer."

She removed one of the tissues from her pocket and wiped her nose while she spoke. Now Khari didn't care what she was saying or what she looked like, she just needed to sit down. She could feel her legs starting to slide from under her and the room began to sway.

"Whoa, hold on to something." Sam dropped his toolbox and hurried over to Khari, putting his arm around her and helping her to the couch. He placed her head on a pillow and tucked a soft knit blanket over her.

"You absolutely should not be making yourself soup or sticking your head in the freezer," he chuckled. "No offense, but you look like death. Just lie still and I'll finish your soup and maybe add something else in with the onion, like food."

"Thank you," Khari whispered, trying to give him a smile, but began coughing instead.

Seeing his kind face breathed luscious ease into her. As much as she hated to be helpless, she knew she was and she surrendered to his offerings. Khari sank herself into the soft couch and listened to the busy sounds in the kitchen. It was impossible for her to smell what Sam was preparing with the massive junk lodged in her head, but she didn't have to smell it to know it would be good. He used to prepare meals for her, always presenting her with a familiar dish made with a new twist. That was Sam, fearless in trying new ingredients and eager to play with flavors to make a good dish better. This trait translated into all that he did.

Lying on the couch, Khari enjoyed the sound of Sam whistling as he cooked. She stared at the front door and tried to breathe quietly out her mouth in between sneezes, wondering what she would say to him. She thought about the last time she and Sam were together in this room, the final time she saw him before leaving for England. The weeks before she left he had seemed edgy and irritable and had gotten worse as her departure day neared. He arrived unannounced at her door the day before her going away party, appearing uncomfortable when she invited him in. He stepped inside and kept his hands in his jean pockets as he spoke.

"I'm sorry I won't be able to make it tomorrow, Khari. I have too many things that need finishing on the ranch." He ran his fingers through his tussled hair before placing them on top of his head. Khari could feel the tension rise from him as he then began rubbing his closed eyes with his thumb and middle finger. She had seen him do that same thing once before when he was worried about his uncle losing his farm.

"It's just a couple of hours. You have to come." She grabbed for his hand and held it tight.

He pulled his hand from hers and looked away as his face turned to stone. He wouldn't look at her and continued staring at the floor. She could see his jaw tighten and his hands were almost one as he squeezed them so tight.

"What is it, Sam? You don't treat me the same anymore. You're ornery and short-tempered. It's not like you," Khari pleaded.

Sam finally left his intense gaze at the floor and peered at her through worried eyes.

"What are you doing, Khari? Why are you traveling to the other side of the world to work at something that isn't you?"

She was shocked and felt the tears rising. She had no idea that he didn't approve of her choice to go.

"You've always supported me in anything I chose to do. All you said was how proud you were of me."

"I know. I *am* proud of you. I will *always* be proud of you. But the fashion world isn't you! Don't you see? There's something else you were meant to do. I can feel it when I look at you. And you're throwing it all away for some foo foo garbage that doesn't mean anything!"

"How dare you, Sam! Why wouldn't you stand by me when I have been so excited to do this? You're trying to bring me down."

"No, I am trying to lift you up. You have amazing talent in art and that is all you used to talk about, but for some reason you pushed all of that away. I watch you on the land, with my horses and in the garden and I see true joy in you when you're with them free to be Khari. Other times I feel there's something you're keeping from me, something that comes between us, and I don't know what it is. It's like you're sad, but you never talk about it. I keep hoping you'll confide in me, but you seem to get farther away from mentioning it."

Khari wiped the tears from her cheeks. She knew he was right, but she couldn't possibly explain all of the turmoil that yanked at her insides—a secret even she didn't understand. She needed to leave to try and escape it, to create a new her with confidence and surety inside. She wanted to tell him, but it wouldn't come out. She didn't want him to think she was crazy. Somehow saying it out loud would be like admitting that she was.

"I need you to be supportive of me going. My goals are different from yours, but that doesn't make them bad. I want to do something important, something that can't be found in this tiny town. I need you to help me, to continue to love me no matter what I do. I have to do this. I have to see what's outside of this house—outside of this town!"

He stared hard at her. The intensity of his eyes bore deep inside of her as he spoke.

"I'm inside of this house, Khari. I'm inside of this town. If that doesn't persuade you to stay, then all of the confusion I am feeling from you must be caused by me."

Without another word, Sam turned and walked out. The storm door banged after him. She felt hurt and betrayed by the one she loved the most and watching him go was like a harsh kick in the gut. But she didn't know what to say to make him happy. She had to go. She had to find peace.

The next night Khari waited for him at the party, her eyes drifting through the crowd of people to the same door he had disappeared through. When he never showed, she watched from her window hoping he would come say good-bye. Every ring of the phone and knock at the door made Khari's heart flinch with hope that he had changed his mind. But he never showed and she left on a sunny clear day feeling dark, grey and lost.

Even now she could feel the emotions of that day and hear the sound of the screen door slam behind him.

"All right. I hope you like vegetable rice soup. I threw in rice and every vegetable I could find, including your friend, the half chopped onion." Sam entered the room carrying a white glass bowl, balanced in the center of a large plate. Steam rose densely from the top. Khari could tell from his smile that he was enjoying himself and this added to her ease. She slid herself up from off the pillow and sat straight enough to eat without spilling down herself. Sam shook a hand towel in the air with sophistication as if it were a linen napkin and laid it gently on her lap causing Khari to chuckle inside.

"Well, I think you'll survive," Sam spoke with a smile. "You just need to eat and rest. I'll be inside the kitchen repairing the window if you need anything." He lingered at her side a moment longer, his eyes drifting momentarily to the steamy bowl on her lap and then to her weepy eyes.

"Do you need anything else?" he finally asked.

The chance to run a brush through her hair and the ability to breathe from her nose came to mind, but she knew he couldn't help her with either one. She found herself wishing she had a reason to keep him near, but couldn't think of one in the moment.

"You've helped me enough. Thank you," Khari said, in her scratchy voice. Tucking a loose strand of hair behind her ear, she raised the bowl from the plate to rest on her chest just under her chin until she could feel the warm steam touching her skin.

"I'll hurry with the window. I'm sure you need to rest without the sound of power tools throbbing in your head. In fact, if you want, I could install it later."

Khari smiled weakly and melted a bit more into the cushions.

"No, please finish. It won't bother me."

As he worked, Khari watched Sam's reflection in the darkened glass door of the sleeping fireplace. Exhaustion and hunger contested for her attention and she found her eyes inevitably closing after every bite. There was comfort in having Sam near. The sound of his hammer, drill, and the low thuds of his struggle with the window actually lulled her. She placed the half-eaten bowl of soup on the floor next to her. She needed to close her eyes, just for a moment...

In between her dreams and reality, Khari opened her eyes when Sam lifted her into his arms. Without energy to protest, she lay limp, and simply allowed him to move her. Deep in a well of fatigue, Khari felt their ascension up the stairs and heard the creak of the boards that were the loudest in front of her bedroom door. The shrill cold when he laid her on her crisp sheets didn't rouse her, and she fell immediately into a needed deep sleep.

Chapter Seven ❧

Khari slept continuously for almost twenty-four hours except for a few visits from her uncle, trips to the bathroom and a small peanut butter sandwich in the late morning. Luckily, the severe aches had almost completely diminished and although it was still impossible to breathe through her nostrils, at least they weren't draining incessantly. She was beginning to feel better.

Although the details were hazy, Khari was sure Sam carried her to bed the night before and thinking on his kindness filled her with quiet gratification. As frightening as it was to open her heart up again, she couldn't help but hope for something more with him. Even the nightmare she had just woken from didn't bother her. She was definitely in danger of giving into her desires to be with him.

She lay attentively listening to the sound of the

breeze through the trees. The rope that hung from the lofty oak tree outside her window swayed and swatted the side of the house. It was a familiar sound, as familiar as the sound of her voice. Uncle Louise had given it to her to use as a large jump rope when she was eight years old, but Khari had been offended at the idea of such a boring use for an object with such potential. She knew immediately that she would hang it from the tall oak close to her window for quick access to the ground below.

After only a couple of days, Khari found her hands covered in painful blisters that made her wince anytime she needed to use them. She tried to hide the sores from her mother, who had warned her against constant use of the rope, by wearing winter gloves, even though it was the middle of summer. Her mother never said a word, but now older, Khari was sure that her mother had known but had kept quiet, realizing she had learned a lesson on her own. Her mother always said that, most of the time, an individual's harshest punishment comes from themselves. She had been right.

This night, in the increasing wind, the sound of the rope's dance was more abrupt and frequent. However, the repetitive noise was not what had awakened Khari, it was the rub of the front wood door opening that had roused her from sleep. At least she thought she had heard it. Her house, that was a moment ago so silent that it seemed to breathe along with her, had been disturbed. It was quiet once more, but Khari was positive she had heard something, and she lay with quickened breath, listening. After several moments of concentration, she conceded to the fact that she had only imagined the noise and closed her eyes once more.

She relaxed and began to drift to Sam's face, when through the stillness the stair creaked. Her heart doubled its beat and she desperately wanted to call out to her mother to inquire if she was home a day early, or to Sam who may have been checking on her in the middle of the night. Was it logical that some unknown person was making their way up the stairs? She was sure she was mistaken, yet began imagining wild scenarios of defense and escape out of sheer panic. When another creak, followed by another, emerged from the stillness, Khari knew she wasn't hearing things.

Her growing fear seemed to magnify every sound in the house, while at the same time impaired her vision. Before she could get out of the blankets she heard the nearing steps end in front of her door. In the moonlight, the outline of a large man stood unmoving, a shape similar to her uncle in height, but larger in the shoulders and thinner in his frame.

Khari leaped from her bed, but her speed caused her to fall to her knees momentarily. She grasped for the lamp from her side table and stumbled awkwardly to the corner nearest the window and farthest from the door where the looming man stood. The open window was her only chance at freedom, but she feared her weakened dexterity would land her on the ground instead of the rope. Still grasping the cold metal of the lamp, she backed into the corner next to the window trying to figure out what was happening.

He spoke without acknowledging her struggle.

"Hello, Khari." His voice was deep, confident and blithe, as if Khari had entered his office for a job interview. The fact that this stranger knew her name left her wondering if he was friend or foe and she waited for him to speak again as she continued inching her quivering body towards the open window.

"I've searched for your family a long time." With a quick jerk of his hand he lifted the light switch, which illuminated the once darkened room in an instant. She squinted at the abrupt light and wondered at how easily he found the switch. She was sick at the thought that he was the one who had rummaged through her room over a week ago, familiarizing himself with her belongings.

"I'm sure you don't know me," he said.

After a few moments, Khari could finally look at him without squinting and was positive that she didn't know him. Appearing to be significantly older than she, he stood straight and dignified, wearing a simple black t-shirt and jeans along with black leather boots. His hair was the same raven color as hers and he wore it long, pulled into a ponytail and braided tight down his back. His jaw was straight and strong, matching the strength of his prominent biceps. Most noticeable though was the tattoo etched down the left side of his face. It began at the tip of his eyebrow and ended at his chin. She may have thought him handsome and noble looking if he wasn't standing before her in such a sinister manner. Now she just considered him ugly and frightening.

How could he possibly know her? Khari stopped

caring and felt her rage intensify at feeling so vulnerable, clinging to the walls of the corner like a mouse before a cat.

"I don't really care who you are, you need to go," Khari said with more confidence than she was feeling. She held the small lamp out in front of her to create a barrier between them.

He snickered as his eyes stared into hers. Khari didn't look away, partly out of fear, partly out of utter disdain.

"I came for an item and I am sure you'll be able to tell me where to find it." He took one step nearer and sat casually at the end of her bed as she inched closer to the window. She was now close enough to feel the breeze. She wished it would carry her away. What could Khari have that was of any value to this man?

"You see, my father knew your grandfather," he began speaking while crossing one leg over the other and pulling a small dagger from his boot. "Unfortunately, they are from the same tribe, which means you and I are from the same tribe. Your grandfather, in a drunken stupor, ranted on about ancient songs and friendly insects that spoke to him, which to any other ears would have sounded like lunacy, but my father knew better. They were pieces to finding the land that he and all of his forbearers craved." He repeatedly turned the weapon over in one hand and ran his thumb across the intricate etchings found on both sides of the blade.

"Regrettably, your grandfather was careless with a very valuable secret. One that my father wanted for himself and would have given anything to have. He included me in the search, and after his death I have continued to hunt. I will accomplish what those who came before me couldn't."

Khari felt her stomach tighten. Friendly insects? Could it be possible that her grandfather sensed the same things that she had for so long? All of the weight, the voices and songs that had saturated her heart and mind her entire life? Had the bees visited him?

Suddenly aware there was so much more going on than she had ever imagined, and that this new knowledge could possibly bring her self-discovery, she momentarily tried to make a connection between herself and her grandfather, but it was futile because she had no recollection of ever meeting him. She attempted to hide the surprise in her face as the stranger stared her down while tapping the silver blade against his raised boot. Unsure of his next move, she lifted the lamp higher. He took a deep breath and stood again moving toward her.

"He had something my father and I both wanted, but it wasn't found after his death, and so we've spent years trying to find it. You see, he kept written pages of his knowledge and experiences, but they were never recovered. All that was found was a photo of two children with the names Katcha and Magpy written on the back. We had encountered them once before, but they disappeared. We never quit searching for the two individuals with those names, never imagining they would have disrespectfully changed them. Finally, we discovered their whereabouts and also found out that he sent them a package a week before his death. But, they had moved and we were forced to look for them all these years." When he spoke, he eyed the room nonchalantly, as if checking for the time.

"I honestly don't know what you're talking about, and I don't care. Just go," Khari said angrily.

She inched another step toward the window. The sheer curtains snaked around her arm in the breeze. She now stood where she needed to in order to climb out. He took a step forward as well and stared at her intently as if trying to figure out if she was telling the truth. His eyes squinted and his head turned slightly. Khari could see his wild grey eyes twitch as he stared through her.

"You have no idea who you are do you?" He snickered as if someone had just told him a joke.

Khari knew her time was up. Keeping the lamp in front of her with one hand, she felt along the windowsill with the other, never removing her steady gaze from him. She needed to keep him talking.

"Whatever writings my grandfather had, they're not here."

His sly face turned to rage in an instant.

"They have to be here, and you're going to give them to me! My father and I made one mistake—we killed your grandfather before we had his writings. I won't make the same mistake again. I will make sure I wait and kill you after you give them to me!"

Khari launched the lamp towards him, but he dodged it easily, fully anticipating the attack. As the lamp crashed to the ground, he lunged for Khari with a wild growl just as she lifted her socked foot onto the windowsill and pushed herself through it and onto the rope in one swift motion. He reached with one hand for her airborne body, but as she had slunk somewhat down the rope, he seized her hair instead. The pull wrenched her head backwards, causing her to nearly lose her grip on the swinging rope. As she clung desperately with her arms and feet, she attempted to wiggle herself free from his grasp, but it was too painful to continue resisting. She knew she needed to try something different.

Instinctively, she remembered something she had heard one of the runway models say she had used against her boyfriend who had begun to mistreat her. Khari reached above her with one hand and pressed her thumb with all her strength into the soft skin between his thumb and finger. He grunted with teeth clenched and released her hair, but she didn't pull her arm away quickly enough, and he gripped his hand tightly around her wrist. Grabbing her arm, he wrenched her toward the window. Khari swung around and pushed against the house with her feet, struggling to free herself, but his hands were strong and determined and didn't loosen. He began lifting her towards the window, but Khari fought back by straightening her legs against the side of the house to keep her distance from him. She tried to hold tighter to the rope, but the sweat from her palm was making it impossible to keep herself from sliding until finally, she could hold onto it no longer. She slipped from the rope and slammed into the side of the tall house, now completely suspended by his grasp on her wrist. He was now free to pull her up. Realizing her desperate situation, she grappled among the brick and mortar for something to hold on to with her free hand and feet.

"Be reasonable, Khari," he sneered. "You're going to fall."

Khari would rather fall than face her fate with this deranged man. Moving her feet, she felt above the kitchen window directly beneath her and her toes found several hollowed out sections in the brick where old mortar had crumbled away. She wedged her sock covered toes into the holes and tried to use her dead weight to resist him. They both struggled for several moments against one another until Khari knew her now stinging toes could not grip the brick much longer. Luckily, his patience ran out before her strength did.

"Have it your way! I'll meet you at the bottom!" he yelled as he released her wrist, sending her falling into the flower garden below. Khari screamed at the searing pain that enveloped her shoulder when she hit the large boulder hidden among the vegetation, but she didn't have time to comfort herself. She knew he was quickly making his way down to her and she would only have seconds to reach the protection of the surrounding trees.

The rainspout had left a large puddle from the storm the day before and she was forced to roll over into the muddy mire to get to her feet, leaving her nightgown and socks covered in mud. She held her injured arm close, trying not to agitate her shoulder as she rushed across the yard. Without looking back, she could hear him exiting the house. The front screen door banged closed, echoing through the stillness. With little time to plan her escape, she followed her instincts and stepped softly across the yard, staying in the shadows. She quickly glanced behind her, but could neither hear nor see him. Regardless, she was aware he was there, somewhere. Finally, she leaped into the dense trees and ran as long and as fast as she could in the darkness. She was unaware of which direction she was headed, but nothing she would encounter in the trees frightened Khari more than the man pursuing her.

The sliver of moon was no help as she struggled to find her way across the expanse and to make out what different shapes and shadows tore and scratched at her. The terrain was mostly flat with occasional ravines and small hills that she was forced to fight her way over. As she ran on, only the collision of her feet against the varied ground and her quickened shallow breath was heard. The pain in her shoulder caused her to groan with every movement as she penetrated the forest deeper and deeper. To Khari, it felt like she had been wrestling her way through the dense vegetation forever, until she finally stumbled into a clearing. Her exhausted broken body and mangled feet could not give her one more inch. Finally, she crumpled to the unruly ground and gave herself to it.

Chapter Eight ❦

Khari woke lying on her stomach in the middle of a field of long grass. The dry tips of the blades brushed together in the wind sending a quiet wave of rushing, like the sound of a nearing rainstorm. A dead tree, bare and still clinging to its roots, lobbed back and forth, croaking as it thumped against a dry straight tree at its side. Each blow of wood against hollow wood matched the pulses of pain that coursed from her brow to her toes.

Khari could scarcely lift her throbbing head from the rough moist ground, but finally succeeded after several tries. She spit out a tiny leaf and specks of dirt from her mouth and slowly brushed her matted hair from her face with her good arm. The feel of her hair reminded her of the way it had been pulled to its limits and she was sure that what she hoped was a nightmare was actually very real. Khari eased her eyes open and lay still, mustering the energy to get herself up. She scanned the space where she now found herself and recalled the happenings of the previous night, disbelieving they had actually occurred. It was difficult to rise to a sitting position without intense pain striking through her shoulder bones and muscles. The impact with the rock was obvious in her now swollen upper arm. She had no choice but to move carefully.

The sun passed in and out of the clouds dancing its light upon her. Only a calm breeze disturbed the silent scene. Khari, wearing close to nothing to protect herself from the elements, shivered at the slight morning chill, grateful winter was long past.

With her strong arm, she straightened herself off the lanky grass and cool dirt and trembled at the pain it caused. The mud that covered her legs, arms and hands had dried. Working like glue, it sealed her torn nightgown and socks tight to her body, leaving it as stiff as the bark that covered the surrounding trees. She tried to peel the cloth away so that she could scratch her now irritated skin, but it pulled too harshly.

Khari rose to her knees and surveyed her surroundings, hoping to decipher her location. It was no use. She had never laid eyes on this field nor the drooping vines and feathery moss suspended from the trees, and she didn't know the direction from which she had come. Fear enveloped her and she felt desperate to find her way back. Her mother would be home soon and would turn frantic in a search for Khari. The deranged man could still be lurking and she needed to warn her. The thought of her mother in his evil hands worried Khari more than anything. What did her grandfather have that was so valuable that people's lives were in danger? Khari mulled over everything the man had said to her about her grandfather and the insects and the ancient songs. The things Khari had worked so hard to escape seemed now to hold greater importance than she had ever dreamed.

Khari felt the need to move, to go somewhere even though she wasn't sure where. She knew she would never make it home if she stayed in the same spot. Holding her injured arm as still as possible with her other hand, she began walking slowly toward the glimmer of sun through the trees, hoping that east was the way she had come.

For hours through thick ivy and over remnant sticks and logs, she stumbled around in an attempt to escape the monotonous surroundings, but nothing ever changed or appeared familiar. She feared she was moving farther from home. Her surroundings felt so foreign, like she was in a different corner of the world, leaving her more empty and frustrated.

With the sun beginning to lower in the cloud-spotted sky, her restless mind tortured her with hundreds of scenarios of what was going to happen and who she was and why the frightening man wanted her family. With each step, she jumped from one thought to the next, contemplating her decision to go away to London and how it had affected her and wondering about the people she had met there. She felt sorry about the way it had ended with Simon, but was mostly vexed with herself. She had no idea who she was, or what she was supposed to do now. She had no interest in college or art, and felt frozen in a nightmare. Exasperated at being lost, and angry at her stamina that was caving under the heavy weight of gnawing hunger and grueling pain, she found herself yearning for Sam.

The varied calls of birds and the scramble of the occasional squirrel or startled deer were Khari's only company among the thick trees. Just as she was about to set herself down on a large rock, feeling mucky inside and out, she spotted a small pond in a clearing, its blue hue so intense it appeared to be stained with pigment. She could see easily through the limpid water to the lifeless logs lying quietly at the bottom and for a moment she wished to be with them. Bits of soft earth surrounding the pond intermingled with fallen pine needles from the large evergreens nearby. She knelt carefully at its edge, lifted water from its resting spot and poured it on her clothing and skin. She continued with the water until her arms and legs were soaked and she could finally loosen her nightgown and socks from her skin. Not caring if it was safe to drink, she guzzled the water quickly until her mouth was moist and she felt refreshed. She stayed still for a moment, allowing the sun to warm and dry her. She once again felt the pressure of her thoughts and emotions pressing down upon her.

What was happening to her? How had she gotten here? Being killed by a deranged man, or starving to death in the middle of the forest, were certainly not worth giving up the spoils of London. And then there was Sam. What was she supposed to do about him coming around and the long forgotten feelings being rekindled? She wished she had never come home.

While she knelt to wash herself, her tangled hair fell past her shoulders exposing the back of her neck to the feel of the breeze. She trembled at its mild touch and turned her wearied face to it, closed her eyes, and inhaled deeply. It wasn't the same air she had breathed a moment ago, but a new gust from a different direction; a warm river of air moving freely through the cooler pockets surrounding it. Its scent was distinct, holding a hint of burning cedar and berries. Khari felt a presence among its movement, which was so familiar and sweet, she wanted to submerge herself in it. It felt like a friend that Khari could trust and confide in.

"Please help me," she whispered. "I don't understand what is happening, or who I am or why I dream of fire and hear voices. But I want to know. Please, I want to know."

Khari sat weeping when around her a sudden shift occurred. The gentle waft of air suddenly changed from calm to chaotic, lifting sticks and leaves around her and sending them into an explosive applause. With this change, something unseen, yet almost tangible, arrived. Khari sensed it around her, but the flying debris kept her from gazing around and so she waited for the disturbance to stop. When it finally subsided, she opened her eyes, intently searching for what she felt was near, but could not see.

She expected to see someone or something, but she discovered she was still alone with the exception of the soft sun glimmering through the high treetops and a large beehive just above her, teeming with buzzing bees. She was perplexed and couldn't understand how she had not seen them before—they were intensely loud and furious. She stared at them fervently, watching the frantic movements of their dance, hoping they were there for her.

For several moments she gazed at them, forgetting her aching shoulder, and hungry middle, and desperately hoped for a connection to the creatures, to hear the hum that she thought she had heard in London. She began to doubt herself when they carried on with their work, seemingly oblivious to her presence. Just when Khari was ready to crumple into herself once more, the bees simultaneously paused into a still mass, leaving only the click of the birds and the waft of the gentle air to be heard. One solitary bee lifted itself from the now silent cluster of the hive into the air and toward Khari, landing silently upon her leg.

She stared at it for a time, but when it stayed still she finally spoke. "Who am I? What's happening to me?" Khari whispered, hoping, finally, for an answer.

In an instant, lavender colored dragonflies accompanied the bees, darting up and down above the still water of the pond just as an array of butterflies intertwined with them, mingling together into one colorful mass. Hundreds of crawlers, including beetles, crickets, aphids and ants escaped their muddy homes and found their way to Khari, surrounding her with gentle grace. Khari was filled with an anxious anticipation at their dance as they enveloped her in a colorful fog; she could see nothing beyond the screen of wild movement.

She was starving for an answer and she knew in this moment she had a chance to finally discover what was happening to her. *Please speak to me* she plead within her heart. At last, the familiar hum that she had longed to hear and was hoping to understand was flowing through the air just as it had in the art gallery thousands of miles away in London.

As its hum carried on, it intertwined and united with the bees', each one creating a different note, combining into one beautiful result. It began softly and then surrounded her with its depth, low, yet magnificent. It seemed to come from the trees, the water, even the rocks and dirt and she felt that she had emerged from a dark tunnel, suddenly enveloped in light. She could perceive everything around her as if peering at it from behind a magnifying glass. Each crack in the earth, every speck of dirt and piece of leaf was before her. In a strange way, she felt that she was the earth and that each object that surrounded her was her own. Amazingly, she could also see a perfect path from where she was to where her home stood. A sense of relief washed through her at seeing her home and knowing where to go. She was no longer confused or frightened and elation replaced any negativity.

The hum continued with the bee still perched upon her, the immense feelings of the grand earth whispered in her soul a secret. *The bees have died to find you. Your land is lost. Your people are lost.*

When the thought seeped into her heart and mind,

she could no longer see her surroundings, but was taken away to a land more beautiful than any she had ever seen. It was guarded by gigantic trees and flat top mountain ranges. Rivers and lakes seeped through the terrain giving life to its teeming foliage.

On a cliff overlooking the land, a man, noble and worn in his face and countenance, stood with a single white feather tucked into his long dark braids. He held a red blanket, stitched with pale symbols encircling a large white pine tree, tight around his shoulders and watched over a large mass of people who were gathered around an enormous living pine, similar to the one woven upon his blanket. It stretched itself high above the ground, and its needles were so pale it shimmered almost white in the sunlight.

Hundreds of people playing, laughing and singing in celebration at its base were too busy to notice another man with his face painted black and ferocious, climbing to the top of the cliff where the regal man stood. The young man with the painted face was influenced by a darkened fiery shadow urging him on as he tore the blanket from old man just before he plunged a knife into his side and pushed him from the jagged edge, leaving him there to die. Khari gasped and sobbed at the horrifying scene, feeling the weight of his death. She watched in horror as his blood seeped over the rocks he fell upon. She cried out in pain and anguish and covered her eyes in an attempt not to witness anymore, but it didn't help. The vision was permeating her heart and mind, not her sight.

Although the scene changed, it did not show joy, but began to manifest the sorrow that passed through the land as they placed their beloved leader in the ground. Khari sensed their struggle to cope. The evil murderous man went before the rest and wickedly tried to pass the blame upon another who was somewhat younger, but favored by the people. The fiery shadow that had lead the wicked young man to kill their leader, now spread like fire and whispered anger into the hearts of the people, leading to a cruel and endless battle. Brothers, sisters and friends became enemies, and began fighting and killing young or old, male or female, and finally scattered from their homes into every direction.

The scene changed to a dusty terrain and Khari recognized the forlorn faces of the same people now in a dry land, each alone, sifting for food through ashes and thorns on hands and knees. Khari could hear their cries even though their faces stayed still and forlorn, never appearing to weep. She knew the cry was from their aching souls, not from their motionless lips, and she cried with them. With uncontrollable sobs, her insides felt as if they would erupt and she finally heaved at the side of the pond and collapsed to the ground. The sight of her people almost decimating themselves was too much for her to handle. A sense of loss overwhelmed her.

She could feel the noble man's sadness and his desperation now as a gentle apparition among the people. His love carried on around them and Khari felt it for her own family as well. She sensed that he loved his people even though he recognized their mistakes and wild ways.

To Khari's relief, the scene changed once more revealing the chief before his death. He had known his life was nearing an end and that his tribe and land were in danger. He knelt in solitude and begged the Great Spirit of all to protect and gather his people if they were separated. Because of the goodness of his heart and the purity of his soul, his desire was granted and he was allowed to choose the land's protectors, the ones he trusted the most: the insects. They became the guardians of the land. It was their task to ensure the land not be found until a descendant was chosen to return.

As the scene ended, Khari realized that her connection to something significant was real and the pulling and nagging she had felt for so long were her people and land calling for her to listen. The voices and fire she had dreamed of so many times were made clear. The influence of hate was as real as the fire that ended up consuming much of their land as they fought one another; it had destroyed and consumed the tribe just the same.

When she was herself once more and in her present surroundings, she remembered all that she had once known as a little girl, but had forgotten. It came upon her like a rush of fast moving water, saturating her spirit and giving her strength as a final thought entered her soul. *Listen and learn. Find your land and your people.*

At first, Khari struggled to believe that she had been chosen for such an important task. Then memories continued to cover her in their deep richness and recalled her desire to be constantly outdoors playing in the soft earth as a child, surrounded by the colorful insects of the earth and sky that she welcomed with her in spite of any trepidation others had toward the creatures. The same hum Khari discerned from the bees emanated from all of the tiny visitors that would come to her with their songs. She remembered them accompanying her daily and how she could understand them, until one summer day when she was twelve, and everything changed.

She had often gone with her mother to work and this particular day was no different. She had strict instructions to stay nearby. It was a home larger than any Khari had encountered, even larger than city hall. It had more space than walls and was filled shamelessly with gaudy furniture and an array of multi-colored and oddly shaped knick-knacks. Following behind her mother, Khari passed through the sprawling estate from the front door to the open backyard where the party was.

She stayed close to her mother and helped her finish setting up the many large porcelain platters and silver bowls full of her finest food. She waited for her mother to turn away before attempting to snatch a favorite pistachio filled cake her mother made on special occasions. When she raised it to her mouth, hoping to devour it in one bite, her mother's knowing voice softly chimed at her from behind. "Thank you for arranging the pistachio cakes so thoughtfully, Khari. You may have one."

Khari let out a sigh, rolled her eyes and returned the round cake atop the nicely arranged platter.

"If you're finished, would you make sure the others have set up fifteen tables exactly, please?"

Without a word, Khari obeyed and weaved her way slowly around the rectangular tables that were placed in boring uniform perfection. Just as she counted fifteen, she caught sight of surrounding blue and yellow beetles that shimmered in the sun at her feet. She picked them up and let them climb onto her arm just as several butterflies and bees arrived as well. There were so many on her arm, it was impossible to see any of her skin. Khari giggled at them, tickled by their movement. Their hum was intense and she sensed that they were trying to tell her something important. Suddenly, a few girls who belonged to the home came behind Khari.

"That's disgusting! You have bugs all over your arm! Bugs like garbage, so you must be garbage!" They laughed and their snickers and whispers stung Khari. Being so isolated her entire life, she had never known such treatment from others. In that moment, Khari stepped outside herself and saw what they saw: an odd, disgusting girl, dirty, with appalling creatures covering her skin. Unsure of how to react, she stayed still until the urge to stop their laughter was too great. She swept the insects from her arm, sending them back to the earth and sky. Her mother must have been embarrassed as well because she passed the rest of the job to her assistant and they quickly left. After that day, she was angry with her tiny friends and refused to listen to their hum any longer, no matter how incessant it was. After a while, they stopped coming to her and Khari tried to make sense of herself and completely forgot about them. But it was no use. Insects or not, Khari had felt a gnawing in her heart ever since.

Sitting in the woods, once again surrounded by insects, she felt shame at having pushed away the ones who were trying to help her people. Had they come to other members of the tribe as well? She couldn't recall her mother or uncle ever having any connection to them, but maybe she never noticed. As Khari was released from her revelry, she stared respectfully at the insects that still surrounded her. It was humbling to realize the bees were leaving the hive, and consequently dying, to help her and her people find their land. They held symmetry much like humans, relying on one another to survive. She felt ashamed at her naive ways and, crying, she begged for forgiveness.

"I'm sorry for not listening. I will find my land and tribe, but how? You've shown me the way home, can you show me how to get to the land?" Khari pleaded.

It cannot be given, it must be found, came the answer within her, just before the insects took to the air and ground once more.

As the ancients departed, Khari rose to her feet and began moving toward her home. She felt enlivened and peaceful. Although the weight that had plagued her for so long had not been lifted, it was given purpose and identity—it was the weight of her people. The whispers were theirs and their beautiful land lay waiting somewhere for them to claim.

Khari's acute sense of her surroundings had not disappeared with the fading of the vision. She was still a part of nature. As she made her way urgently toward home, the sun fell below the trees, leaving her in darkness. The same darkness that had frightened her the night before, she now welcomed with confidence. She was light on her feet as she was a part of her world, instead of a stranger fighting her way through it. Finally, in her dirt covered skin, she felt beautiful, and holding tight to her past, she knew her path.

Chapter Nine ❧

The red and blue lights flashed wildly in front of Khari's house. She emerged from the trees, relieved to see her Uncle Louis comforting her mother as they spoke with police officers. Her mother's hands covered her face as she wept. Khari's bedroom light was on and a couple of officers stood in the window, while others caroused the grounds with flashlights searching for what she assumed was her, or signs of her.

She wasted no time revealing herself, calling to her mother as she passed quickly across the grass. Upon hearing Khari's voice, everyone paused their efforts and turned to watch her emerge from the dark trees. She was met with urgency. Khari cautioned them about her hurt arm as her mother carefully covered her in ecstatic hugs and kisses before ushering her quickly into the house. Louis and police officers trailed behind.

Upon entering the house Khari immediately noticed the upheaval of items everywhere, from books in the hall, to dishes in the kitchen, everything was in disarray. She imagined the man, angry at her escape, attempted to find the book on his own. It made her stomach sick to think of his livid determined eyes. The sound of his cruel voice rang in her head. She tried not to think about him, focusing instead on the relief that he was gone. She sat on the couch, soothed by the feel of the soft blanket her mother had wrapped around her shoulders, and sipped water slowly from a glass.

An officer barraged her with questions while one of the medics jumped from the newly arrived ambulance and began attending to the cuts on her body and wrapping her injured arm tight against her middle with white cloth. They asked her personal questions—her name, what year it was; general inquiries to make sure she was who they thought she was and that her mental state was normal. The incessant questions kept her from asking her family what she wanted to know, which made her feel increaseingly anxious.

"Khari, could you explain in detail what happened?" inquired one of the officers.

He was a large round man, with a mustache that covered his upper lip entirely and a voice that was higher than it should have been for having such sizable stature. He studied Khari over his lowered spectacles as she went into detail about her illness, beginning with when she was sleeping. In between Khari's sentences, the storm door swung open with sudden severity and Sam pushed his way through. He looked extremely distraught with his hair disheveled and oil covering his hands. From the amount of grease that was streaked across his faded blue t-shirt, he appeared to have come directly from underneath a leaky car. Khari thought he was about to start yelling until his eyes met hers and he relaxed a bit, slightly embarrassed at everyone staring at him.

"I heard Khari was in trouble. I came to see what I could do to help," he said before nearing Khari.

"Are you all right?" he asked her.

Khari couldn't help but smile at seeing his worried oil-streaked face.

"Yes. I am now," she answered, hoping her hovering uncle would move away and let Sam sit next to her.

"Have a seat, Sam." Khari's mother offered him a wet rag and directed him to an empty chair across the room. He sat on its edge and began wiping his filthy palms on the cloth as he silently mouthed the question, "Are you sure you're okay?" toward Khari.

Khari nodded and smiled. He smiled back, sending what felt like thousands of butterflies through every inch of her.

"Please continue," the plump officer said, annoyed by the interruption.

Khari recounted everything, from being awakened by squeaks of the floor to escaping out the window.

"So you say you heard the front door open? Did you leave it unlocked?"

Khari glanced at Sam. "Sam was here the night before and shut the door behind him."

"Did you lock it, son?" asked the officer turning around to look at Sam.

Sam didn't hesitate in his answer. "Yes sir. I'm positive I did."

"Well, apparently the culprit has a key. Any idea where he might have gotten it?"

Khari's mom stepped from out of the kitchen where she was making Khari a quick sandwich. "We had another break-in recently. I'm sure it was the same man. I didn't notice a house key missing in the mess he left, but he must have taken one."

"It would probably be a good idea to change the locks. Did he say what he was after?" the officer asked, not looking up from his scribbling on the small notebook.

Khari was reluctant to answer, unsure about what her family knew. "He said...he wanted some of my grandfather's writings." Khari glanced at her uncle when she said it. His face winced into a mix of anger and disgust.

"Did you have what he wanted?" The officer raised his eyes to peer at Khari without moving his head.

"No. I had no idea what he was talking about, but he didn't believe me."

"Well, we will put out a search for the man you described and see if we can find him before he does return. I don't need any more from you, but please call us if you think of anything else that might assist us in our efforts. Good evening." With that, her mother walked the officers outside while answering questions about the house. The room cleared of the rest of the uniformed individuals until Khari was left alone with Louis and Sam.

Louis turned to her and spoke with a forced grin on his face, obviously trying to reassure Khari.

"I'm sorry you had to go through all of this, Khari," he said, peering at his feet and nervously twisting his toothpick before shifting it to the opposite corner of his mouth.

"Uncle Louis, I don't know who that man was, but he knows who we are. He talked about you and my mom and even about grandfather. What's going on? Do you know him?" Khari could see his face change from supportive, to flushed with angst. His gruff voice scratched a little as he tried to speak in a whisper.

"Yes. I know who he is." He rubbed the back of his neck appearing uneasy. "His name is Catunta. Your mother and I have tried to protect you from him your entire life. Unfortunately that included not telling you many things. We were hoping this day wouldn't come, but it seems it has and it's time we tell you what we know."

Khari's mother entered the room, turning to close the door behind her.

"Well, Khari, they definitely think your shoulder is broken and they want you to go immediately to have it taken care of."

"Mom? What secrets have you been keeping from me?" Khari asked sullenly.

Her mother paused with her hand still gripping the doorknob, her back toward Khari. After a moment, she closed the door, breathed deep and turned around to look Khari in the eyes. Khari could see a disquiet that she had never witnessed in her mother's face. Lines began to gather in her forehead and her mouth turned down. She sat on the other side of Khari.

"I'm sorry, Khari. There are things I never told you. I've been trying your entire life to keep you from harm. Louis and I were hoping that Catunta wouldn't find us and that there would never be a need to tell you that he killed your grandfather and that he was hoping to do the same to us."

Khari was speechless and stared at her mother in disbelief.

Louis interjected. "After your grandfather's death, I watched Catunta closely, knowing what he and his father Amaro had done to him. But I was never able to prove it." Her uncle spoke quietly, his brown eyes filled with intensity. It was unnerving for Khari to see him so serious, he was always so fun loving and quirky. "The authorities called it a suicide since he was found hanging in a noose, with a stool knocked out from under him and a bottle of rum broken on the floor underneath. But, your mother and I knew better. We received a large envelope a week before that included his diary of sorts and a note about Amaro and his increasing demands to know the location of our people's land. Somehow, Grandfather Tula had met up with Amaro and they had become friends when they learned they were from the same tribe. It was unheard of to find another person from our long ago scattered Madakan tribe and he was so excited."

Khari interrupted. "Madakan? That's our tribe's name?"

"Yes, and my father gave me the tribal name Cacha and your mother's is Magpy. We changed our names to hide ourselves from Catunta."

"Do I have a tribal name?" Khari interjected.

"I gave you an important name in a different language," her mother said cautiously. "Kharishma means miracle and that's what you were. I really didn't have the knowledge of the language to give you a tribal name. Plus, I wanted to hide you from Catunta."

"I've never heard of another member of our tribe besides Catunta and Amaro, but I'm sure they're out there," Louis said. "My father felt like he was supposed to find our people, but he had trouble with alcohol that kept him from it. He tried to cover up his difficult childhood with the nasty stuff and when our mother died, it intensified."

Khari could tell by the distant look in his eyes that it was difficult for Louis to talk about.

"He was one of the most genuine, compassionate people I knew," Louis continued, "even though his depression seemed to overpower him. When he was sober, he would tell us stories of our tribe and their destruction, and of the last leader, Chief Arancaya who lead the people with more love than any other ever known, until the day he was murdered."

"Yes. I've seen him," Khari stated without hesitation, peering at her feet. She was ready to talk about what she had seen and who she was. It seemed right on her tongue ready to burst out in the open, even though the fear of telling the truth made her stomach squirm. She glanced at

Sam wondering how freaked out he was to hear all of this. After all, he was the one she had always feared to tell. Having him think less of her pained her greatly. So far he appeared unfazed, listening intently while continuing to rub at the oil covering his hands.

Khari continued slowly. "He was murdered on a high cliff overlooking a beautiful land. But, he was so good and so pure in his heart, the Great Spirit granted his desire to protect his land and unite his people. However, he didn't trust any human in his tribe to reconcile and protect the land and so he actually looked for help from the creatures that he knew were wise and long living, who understood man and their workings, but would not be persuaded by riches or power or taking the land for their own kind. They already shared its space and held realms of their own deep in the earth and in the space of the air."

She knew the next part would be hard to believe and she paused before continuing.

"The ones he chose were the insects or Ancient Ones. They have been on this earth since the beginning of its creation and are now in charge of helping our people find one another and our land. I've heard their songs my entire life and felt the presence of our land and people. Only, I just didn't know it."

Sam appeared stunned, yet engrossed in every word. "Why didn't you ever say anything?" he questioned.

"I'm sorry," Khari said. "Even now, with all that I know, it's hard for me to talk about. My whole life I felt isolated and honestly, kind of like a lunatic. I couldn't ever shake this unseen annoyance around me. Sometimes it wasn't very strong even though it followed me everywhere, even around the world. I never talked about it because I was embarrassed and I knew I couldn't explain what was going on inside of me even if I wanted to. I'm sorry I didn't confide in you." Khari kept her gaze on him.

"It's okay. It's actually a relief to know it wasn't me you were running from." They exchanged smiles and she felt a jolt of excitement bound within her. Her secret was out and nobody was running. Had her mom felt the same things?

"Mom...Louis...have either of you felt what I described to you? Can you hear the insects?"

Khari gazed at her mother and uncle as she waited for what seemed like an eternity for an answer.

Instead of responding right away, they exchanged long glances toward one another. Her mother answered first.

"We've never experienced what you've gone through, but someone close to us did. Your grandfather had the same ability and feelings as you. The insects would communicate with him. They would connect him to the earth, to our people's land. He could hear them, but, no, we can't. He taught us that the last great chief of our tribe had the gift as well and that every chief before him did, too. It was something only certain individuals were blessed with."

"Since my earliest memories, I've heard them. But...what does that mean?" She turned to her mother finally sitting on the other side of her.

"Mom, did you know that I could hear the insects?"

Khari's mother shut her eyes for a moment as tears began to cascade down her face.

"Yes. I've always known. I used to watch you speaking and singing with them all of the time."

Khari felt her face get hot as she stared at her mother in disbelief.

"If you knew who they were and my special connection to them, why didn't you ever tell me? Especially when I rejected them?"

This was the first time Khari had ever felt betrayed by her mother and it was difficult for her take in. She bit her bottom lip and squeezed her eyelids tight to stop the tears, but they welled up in her eyes, finally spilling down her cheeks. Her heart was weakened. Her mother took her hand, but Khari couldn't bear to be touched and pulled it away.

"I'm so sorry, Khari. I only wanted to protect you. In fact, Catunta came close to finding us a couple of times. The last one was at a great estate where we had gone to cater a party. He showed up as a guest and we had to make a run for it. You had your arm covered with the insects and were surrounded by some girls. It was wrenching for me to ignore what I saw happening with you. I wanted to help you feel better, but I knew your ignorance about the insects and the land was my only chance to save you from Catunta's grasp."

Khari remembered that day and how the hum of the insects was intense as they were trying to tell her something. Now it made sense that they were trying to warn her of Catunta's presence and that's why her mother wanted to leave so quickly.

"So you weren't embarrassed by me?" Khari asked.

"Oh, never, Khari. Forgive me. I couldn't tell you who you were and have you accidentally say something to someone that would give Catunta a chance to find us. You were so young and it would have been too much for you to handle. The stress on me hiding you away was so great and I never wanted you to feel any of that fear. As you grew and he didn't find us, I always looked for the right time to tell you, but never found one."

Khari stared at the floor listening and trying to work out what her mother was telling her, but the hurt spread through her and clouded her thinking. Her voice rose as she spoke, "You don't understand. I went through life never understanding what was happening to me and running from who I was. I have felt like a freak more than you can imagine, not just from the insects communicating, but from the dreams, songs and whispers I hear constantly. Our people and land, have been talking to me, and I never understood because nobody guided me. You can't expect me to be okay with that. And then you let me leave half way around the world."

"I'm so sorry, Khari. My mistake, and one I will forever regret, is feeling relieved when you stopped listening and found interest in something that I knew would keep you from the danger of Catunta. Every time I saw you communicating with them I held my breath and wondered if that was the time they would lead you into the danger of looking for our land. That is how your grandfather died and I couldn't have that happen to you too. As sad as I was to part with you when you went away to England, I felt relief that you were far from possible danger."

Khari didn't want to discuss anymore about how betrayed she felt in front of Sam. He must have already been shocked by everything else he was hearing. She swallowed hard.

"So how was Grandfather similar to me?"

Her uncle continued. "We know you have the same ability to communicate with them, just as your grandfather did. We don't really know what he heard from them, but he did write some things down."

Khari dried her face, feeling confused. She tried to think of any clues she may have had that would help her find the land, but she had only seen it without any knowledge of where it was. "Did he find the land?"

Khari's mother answered. "As far as we know, he didn't know where it was. He apparently heard many songs and saw our people and land in visions. Unfortunately, he lacked the confidence or will to find out what it all meant. He told us stories growing up of a lost land, and he wrote down much of what he knew in a book that he kept tucked inside of his shirt, which, for some reason, he considered the safest place." She raised her eyebrows and smiled before continuing.

"We aren't sure what he ever truly understood. He knew that the chief would be called to find the tribe, yet your grandfather had difficulty understanding the whole picture. He seemed to be weighed down by the idea of how to accomplish the calling of chief and the gathering of his people. He felt he wasn't good enough to fulfill such a great task and only drank more from the anxiety and guilt."

Khari felt a prick inside at hearing two words as if they were the only two uttered: *gathering* and *chief.*

"Wait. So, if the chief of our tribe hears the hum of the insects, does that make me...?"

"Chief? Yes." Her uncle smiled a boyish smile when he said it, as if it was a funny joke.

Khari choked as her throat felt like it was closing off. She swallowed hard.

"I knew you were meant to do great things," Sam said, giving her a wink.

"I can't be chief. Shouldn't the calling of chief be passed on to one of you? Why has it skipped to me? Can a woman even be chief?" Khari asked excitedly, moving to the edge of her seat.

"It's rare for a woman to be chief, but it's happened in other tribes. It's said that the gift skips a generation, which is why you have it," Louis said. "I think some things are planned even before we are born and we don't always know why. You were chosen for a reason and now you have a choice just as your grandfather did."

Being chief surpassed a hundred jobs with Launa. Khari began to feel a little sick to her stomach at the responsibility laid before her. She hadn't the faintest idea where to begin, but she knew it was time to see her grandfather's writings.

"So, where is his diary? Crazy Catunta has been

through our house twice. Do you think he found it?"

Her mother's eyes shined. "Not a chance. It's in our very best hiding place."

The attic was nearly impossible to detect unless one looked closely from the outside and noticed the small circular window high above the front door, directly over Khari's mother's room. It was the only window to the attic, the single indication that the small space existed. From inside the house, its entrance was practically impossible to see.

Across from Khari's room, inside her mother's office, the walk-in closet was lined with thin metal shelves jammed full of shoeboxes and filing folders. There, amid the clutter, was an unseen door leading to the highest floor. The old light in the center of the closet still clung to a string. One gentle pull of the string and the light would click on. One heavy pull to the point where one would expect the thin string to break, the ceiling would lower, revealing old wooden stairs leading up to the attic. It was made with such genius that the lines of the opening appear to be nothing more than ceiling tiles connecting with one another. It was there where the notebook was lying amongst the sheet covered mounds and dust of the secret loft.

When she was young, Khari imagined the priceless wonders the builders of the home must have owned to warrant such workmanship. She would sit inside its walls and imagine the gold and jewels that were surely once hidden in the simple space.

After Sam hugged Khari good-bye and reassured her all of the new discoveries were amazing, he rushed back to help his uncle lift the engine from his car. Along with her mother and uncle, Khari made her way to the attic through the mess of papers and boxes strewn inside the closet. Catunta had found his way to the secluded space and must have rummaged desperately through the clutter, never knowing what was hiding just above his head. Thinking about his frustration gave Khari a great sense of satisfaction and she reveled in the feeling long after they had entered the dank and dusty attic space.

Without hesitation, her mother removed the sheet covering the wooden trunk that held her most precious items and lifted the heavy lid. Khari held her breath, waiting anxiously to hold the important writings. It felt like forever that her mother searched through the trunk's contents before finding it.

Finally, Khari held it in her hand, feeling completely disappointed and baffled. The imagined grandeur of the all-important writings that Khari visualized—bound with the finest materials, mysterious symbols possibly etched in gold lettering—fell flat when she stared at the blue spiral notebook that lay like a joke atop her shaky palms. Khari was about to ask her mother if she was kidding until she noticed the name written crudely with black pen: *Tula*, her grandfather's tribal name. She ran her fingers over his name written in deepened lines across the glossy cover. An immediate connection to her grandfather and the book ran through her. This had to be the key she had been hoping for.

Chapter Ten ✤

Dressed in jeans and a t-shirt, Khari leaned comfortably against the foot of the willow tree studying the blue notebook in her hands. She was oblivious to the bees buzzing about her; butterflies in her loose hair; lazy beetles and ladybugs resting against her naked dirt covered feet. Sam's nearing footsteps broke her concentration.

"Oh hey!" Khari stopped reading and plopped the notebook onto her stomach. She straightened herself against the trunk and curled under her pink painted toes before pushing them deeper into the delicate earth. The movement stirred several butterflies to flight.

"It's refreshing to see you under this tree with dirty feet. You look happy," Sam said as he sat next to her. "And, I'll bet you're ecstatic to have your cast off. " Sam lifted Khari's arm, moving it back and forth as if testing a hinge. "How does it feel?" he asked with a smile.

"I feel lighter, that's for sure," Khari chuckled. His warm hands on her arm sent a surge of sparks through her.

"And are your friends speaking to you today?" He grinned, motioning to the insects that had laid themselves gently upon her. An occasional bee came and went while others scoured the flowers nearby. She lifted a praying mantis that clung to her arm and held it in her hand.

"I guess so. They don't really speak to me with words. It's more like a quiet drone that I sense from them whether they are next to me, or hiding in the trees, or in the ground. But, when they communicate a thought with me, it's louder than when they're just hanging around. It's kind of like the difference between the sound of an engine idling and when it's moving. It's basically the same sound, but at times one is very quiet and other times it bellows."

"That makes sense. I think it's amazing that you have the ability to understand them. You're full of special surprises." He gazed at Khari hard and long. Khari smiled, feeling her cheeks get hot. It felt good to hear that her relationship with the insects didn't scare him.

"It's nice to know my purpose with them and that I'm not crazy." Khari couldn't help the rising sting at the thought of her mother and uncle lying to her for so long. She placed her hair behind her ear and tried to push the reality away. Her hand brushed against his and she wished she had a reason to touch it again.

"So, how is your reading going? Any clues?" he

asked gazing at the notebook pages.

Khari placed the mantis on the ground next to her and shrugged. She was reluctant to answer his question and be torn from the serene feelings that she enjoyed just a moment ago in his presence. She had felt alone and heavy with the notebook's weight. Weeks passed and her body was whole again, yet her spirit waned. Khari had scrutinized its crisp pages repeatedly, beginning in the hospital while she awaited x-rays and a cast, and finishing at home, recuperating from her ordeal. The only relief from her intensely idle feelings and awkward one-armed activity was visits from Sam, and reading the contents of the notebook. She hoped with each page that something would guide her, yet instead, she felt farther away from any answers.

The writing was nearly illegible and much of what was written was either irrelevant or cryptic. Tula's sentences were often erratic and it was easy for Khari to decipher when he had been writing sober and when he had been drunk. When thoughts were random and words merely scrawled, she knew he was not himself. But other pages were clear and the beauty of his language transformed a simple thought into a beautiful scene, like organizing random notes into an amazing piece of music. When she read these genuine pages she could see distinct images before her, as if she were truly there. Yet seeing them was different than understanding them and Khari struggled under the heavy burden of deciphering. One thing she knew for certain—Tula felt lost in his world and it pained her to read his sadness.

With how frustrating it was not to understand, she wouldn't give up. She knew there had to be something there to help her or Catunta wouldn't have wanted it so badly. She wouldn't give up searching it for answers.

Khari considered not telling Sam all of the daunting details, but she looked into his empathetic eyes and couldn't help but confide in him.

"Honestly, I'm feeling frustrated like I'm trying to construct a puzzle whose pieces don't fit together. I'm lost every time I read his writings. I can't figure them out Sam. I feel stuck. There are such beautiful visions he recorded, but like my dreams, they are all hazy and I'm having a hard time deciphering them. There are similarities to scenes of the past that I have already witnessed, like the man with the black painted face, the white pine tree and the fire. Then there are parts that are completely foreign, like rocks placed in patterned lines and words to songs; it's all so unsettled. I'm not sure I'll ever be able to make sense of it." It was so refreshing to discuss the details and emotions that she had kept secret for so long, that she didn't care that she was rambling.

"Have you ever had a thought on the edge of being uttered, but then it fades away and suddenly you can't remember what it was you were thinking? Like your brain is playing games with you? I feel that way all of the time, like the understanding is there, it's just teasing me, fading in and out of my mind. I can sense obscure voices in the background, but they're blurry, so I can't understand them. Yet, the mumbling continues."

Khari noticed a grin on Sam's face as he watched her

speak. "You think I'm crazy don't you?"

"What? There is no way I think you're crazy. Lovely, yes. Crazy, no. You're far from crazy."

"But you're smirking at me." She narrowed her eyes at him.

"That's not why I'm smiling, I swear. I'm just happy to listen to you. It's refreshing to see how passionate you are. I always felt you held something extra important inside of you. I could see a light brighter in you than in any other person I've ever known. When it began to fade, it scared me. I feel that a lost friend has returned and listening to you is wonderful."

Sam placed his hand on hers and pressed it with a reassuring grip. Khari felt ridiculous to think that he could have been laughing at her. He had been her dearest friend long before she left for London. Around him she felt like a better person than she was.

"You're nowhere near being insane. You'll figure it out. Don't worry, just try not to think too much, you'll frighten the answers away. Let them come to you." Sam smiled. "And definitely take breaks more often." His summer colored skin brightened his light-colored eyes. Khari wondered as she looked at him, if he worked at charming her, or if it just came naturally.

With it so late in the afternoon she was sure he had finished work for the day, and her heart lifted at the chance of uninterrupted time with him, but desperately hoped he was not about to ask her to go to the town festival. Her mother tried to persuade her to go before she left to set up her food booth. Khari couldn't bring herself to say yes, with so much going on within her, she couldn't possibly smile and socialize.

"I thought, maybe with your arm healed you'd like to take a ride."

"A ride? What kind of ride?" Khari raised an eyebrow his way.

"It's a surprise."

Sam picked up the notebook and stood up before offering Khari his hand. She took it and he lifted her to her feet. As they made their way down the grassy hill to the back of the house he simpered charismatically,

"Let's just say someone misses you." He grinned.

It didn't take long for Khari to figure out who he was talking about. *Ember.*

Sam's home lay east on the border of town where the thick trees intertwine with the long grazing grasses. It was ideal land for the hundreds of cattle and horses that carouse the property within the surrounding wood fencing. As they pulled up to Sam's ranch, the endless fields of green lush grass at the foot of the gentle hills welcomed them. Within the fiery light of the nearly descending sun, Khari could see the many horses within the gates grazing; a few playing, eating and resting.

Khari's spirit rose as they exited the car in front of the majestic mass of colored horses.

Sam's quick high-pitched whistle caused the horses to stir. Khari stayed near Sam and waited, worried Ember would not remember her as she searched the group for him. Her arm touched Sam's and she grasped his index and middle fingers that rested on the fence. He spoke to Khari reassuringly, "Don't worry. He'll remember you. After all, you were practically his mother when we brought him here so young. Your bond isn't so thin that a year could break it."

"What makes you think I'm worried?" Khari rebutted.

"You always grasp my two fingers when you're worried."

Khari, unaware of her action, let go embarrassed and searched through the horses once more.

"Sorry, I didn't realize."

"Don't apologize for something that I enjoyed." He winked at her and smiled. Khari returned the grin.

As the greater herd of horses parted somewhat in their movement, Khari spotted a horse, deep black and shiny, like the feathers of a crow. He stood shaking the dust from his mane before his eyes caught Khari's. She could hardly breathe. She flashed a look at Sam.

"Go on Khari, he's not sure it's you."

Khari slipped off her sandals and lifted herself over the wooden fence, dropping roughly into the damp earth and scratchy grass. To Khari, its cool touch was as refreshing as water. She never entered the corral with shoes. She could connect to the earth and its creatures better without the distracting barrier.

After only a few steps toward the majestic animal, the horse pawed at the mud fiercely and then paused, gazing her way once more. Khari stopped as well and waited. The only sound was from the movement of the other horses as they paraded around aimlessly at the sight of her in their midst.

Just before Khari was about to call to the dark horse, he reared up and broke into a sprint toward her, finally encircling her with his rhythmic steps and lifting his front legs from the ground repeatedly. Khari laughed out loud at his childlike gestures. Relieved that he knew her, she held out her hand with her palm down. It was a sign she used since he was young to tell him when she was ready to ride. Ember brayed and slowed, ceasing his joyful romp and trotted swiftly to her side. She lovingly caressed his cheekbones and kissed him on his muzzle.

"Hello, Ember. You didn't forget me. I'm sorry I disappeared for so long. Life has been really strange." Ember's hot breath blew the stray hairs from Khari's cheeks just before he nudged her.

"Do you want to dance?" she questioned softly to which Ember dropped his front leg and neighed in response. Khari looked back at Sam as he was placing a saddle upon a chestnut colored mare. He lifted his head toward her. "I'll catch up. You two are fast, but you haven't seen our new moves."

Khari tightened her fingers around Embers wiry mane and with one swift movement, bounded naturally onto his soft back.

"You sure you won't use one?" Sam questioned motioning to his saddle that he buckled tightly to the horse.

Sam had taught her to ride long ago and always

prodded her to use a saddle. But, she never enjoyed riding with one and would not give into his coaxing. Without one, Khari could sense Embers next move like a hand inside a glove that fit perfectly together and moved in sync.

"Are you crazy? And fall off before we reach half way? No thanks. Oh, and sorry in advance for the dust cloud you're about to eat." Khari taunted.

"We'll see who's eating whose dust," he rebutted.

She caressed Ember's large neck, smoothing over the tensed muscles before positioning her head low behind his. She tightened her fingers through his mane and her legs around his back, lifting her feet up behind her. Ember seemed to shake with excitement, barely able to stay still. He shifted and brayed with heavy breath as Khari readied herself.

"Ready Ember?" she whispered in his twitching ear. She lowered her head even more until the tips from his coarse mane tickled her chin and the ends of her hair hung over his back.

"Lets dance!" Khari hollered and Ember took off as if the strike of a whip had laid itself across his backside. He was in a full sprint through the open space. Accompanying the thud of hooves against the ground was a now distant cheer from Sam that rang from behind them.

The wind blew wildly through her hair and she felt lifted into the air as if they were birds synchronized in flight. Ember's gallops were smooth across the ground, nearly unfelt as if he never made contact with the hard earth; his stride graceful and effortless.

As Khari and Ember neared the edge of the expansive field, Sam and his horse caught up, racing along side them. Sam whooped and yelped in their direction, calling them on.

"Come on Ember! We can't let them beat us!" Khari called, sending Ember faster across the terrain just as the sun disappeared behind the hills. The hues of the land in shades of green were more vibrant and clear in the changed light and the air cooled.

Sam caught up and kept pace with them until they neared the fence. He slowed and began to turn away from the wooden obstacle, preparing to race back in the other direction just as Khari and Ember picked up speed and leaped flawlessly over the fence, landing perfectly on the other side. They slowed and turned, trotting proudly back.

"You know, Chester and I never covered jumping fences. I would say that would be considered cheating," Sam called to her.

"Hey, I never told you not to teach him to jump. Besides, there's a nice wide gate only feet away you could open and slide easily through and then we could keep racing."

"Okay then. If I beat you to the tree in the far corner, we go to the last of the town festival tonight."

"My mother already tried to talk me into going. But, I accept the challenge. I hope you have alternate plans for tonight."

Sam turned his horse before he headed back toward

her and leaped over the fence with ease.

"Oh! Faker!" she said.

"Do you need a head start?" Sam eyed her with a playful gaze.

"I was just about to ask you the same thing." They both hunkered down upon their steeds cautiously eying one another.

"Well, since neither one of us needs a head start, there's nothing more to do than, GO!" Sam yelled as they sped off from their resting places careening quickly towards the solitary tree standing yards away.

The beat of hooves was simultaneous and created a deep boom as they crossed the wild grassy pasture that was thick and flourishing from growing unrestrained. Sam pulled ahead of her just enough that she could catch a glimpse of him. With the darkness swallowing the dimmed light, it left a dusky atmosphere and Khari couldn't help but notice the way Sam almost glowed within it.

Droves of memories of the many hours they had spent on his ranch were brought back at the sight of him riding. She realized how much she had truly missed him. When they were younger, her feelings for him were so tiny and new. Now, tearing across the land by Sam's side, she realized how those fresh and tender sentiments had dug deep and strengthened within her as would the roots of a giant tree expanding and swelling within the ground it's anchored to. She was unsure how or when it had happened, but she could feel it full inside of her. She was terrified at the realization. She couldn't bear being hurt by him again and she wasn't sure if he still held those disappointed feelings toward her. If he knew about Simon, he could have given up on her long ago.

Her deep thoughts had distracted her from the race. Sam had reached the tree several strides before her and was trotting his horse around the tree gloating.

"Well, I must say you looked intent on something other than reaching the tree. I hope you won't ask for a rematch, I've ran Chester pretty hard."

Khari came back to the current moment and realized she had lost, which her competitive side always disliked. Surprisingly, she couldn't care less and smiled at him.

"Of course not, you won a fair race. It looks like you get to take me to the festival after all."

Khari sat at the edge of her bed in a muted blue dress and her favorite brown leather boots. She awaited Sam's arrival feeling nervous for more reasons than one. Not only was she supposed to go on a real date with Sam for the first time since she had returned from London, but she was anxious that she would not be any fun.

Her grandfather's notebook felt heavy and daunting in her hand. She tossed it carelessly on the bed and took several deep breaths. She told herself to be calm. She knew her heart was heavy, but she decided to try and forget her worries for Sam's sake. He had been so patient with her and shown her nothing but friendship and kindness. She wanted to give him the same in return. She had to try and forget the craziness going on. There was no denying that there was still an underlying awkwardness that neither Khari nor Sam had acknowledged outwardly yet. Maybe the night would allow some mending to take place between them.

The sound of popping rocks under heavy wheels signaled Sam's arrival. Anxious not to leave him waiting, she slid the notebook under her mattress, brushed quickly through her hair and grabbed a light sweater. She bolted the new locks on the door before meeting Sam at his truck.

He was holding the door open, dressed in dark jeans and a crisp white button-up shirt that was loosely tucked into his indigo jeans. His dark brown belt and his shiny black boots finished it off. Laying eyes on him sent instant gratification through her and calm entered her heart. It was suddenly easy to forget the stress she was under and relax in his presence.

"There she is. Are you ready for some serious sugar, incessant noise, and incredible dancing?"

"I've seen your dancing, and I'm not sure *incredible* quite describes it," Khari teased as she stepped up inside his truck with nothing more than a slight hop. He closed the door behind her and entered in on the other side.

"It's been a long time since we've danced together. You really shouldn't judge so hastily. I've learned some new steps that may surprise you."

"Oh, I am fully ready to be surprised," she retorted with a smile as they began the drive into town.

Summer Festival took place at the end of each

summer, no matter the weather. One year, it rained sheets, but nobody cared. All festivities were simply divided into surrounding stores. The food contests relocated into the restaurants, games into the grocery store, while the flower judging took place in the antiques shop, and the dancing, which carried on the longest, took place in city hall. Nothing ever ruined the festival. It was a night oozing with tradition, down to the crumbs of the cake varieties and the notes of the unvarying songs. Every detail remained unchanged after so many years.

As they parked and entered the crowded streets, Khari hoped that they would have at least missed the chicken dance so she wouldn't feel obligated to join in. She always had the excuse of helping her mother serve food in her beans and bread booth during previous years, but now there was no reason for her not to participate. To her dread, they hadn't missed it and the moment they arrived her uncle and others summoned them onto the makeshift wooden dance floor, which was raised just over the courtyard benches in the middle of town. Square lanterns and tiny lights dangled overhead which began to brighten as the sky faded into hues of orange and red.

Khari protested emphatically to the crowd's pleadings and stepped toward her mother's booth, ready to use helping her as an excuse not to participate. Sam held his hand out towards her.

"Now, how can I show you those moves if you won't let me?" He turned and grinned at her.

"I don't think those moves were supposed to include imitating poultry," Khari responded, folding her arms and trying to ignore the now rhythmic chanting of the crowd calling her name.

"Fair enough. But how can you say no to your faithful fans?" he asked as he pointed his thumb back in their direction. Khari figured being obstinate and creating a scene was more embarrassing than the dance.

"Persuasive, aren't you?" Khari took his hand and whispered in his ear, "You owe me chocolate. Lots of chocolate."

They made their way up the stairs and onto the dance floor as the crowd cheered and welcomed them. Many approached Khari and commented they were glad she was back and that she was all right. One older woman even whispered in Khari's ear with a wink about how charming British men are. Khari chuckled uncomfortably just as the playful music started, grateful Sam had not heard.

With the music blaring, everyone began to dance. Khari was unsure of all the steps, but made an effort to let her apprehensions go and move to the quick music. It was a silly dance that required no coordination and even though this was Khari's first time dancing the chicken dance, she began to recall every silly move from years of watching. Khari found herself with Sam trying to outdo him with every movement as the beat got faster and faster. Sam caught on to her plan and strengthened his moves as well. Within moments of back and forth dancing, Khari forgot that she didn't want to be there and danced with fervor. They graced each other with laughter in between each movement and finally feeling the heat of the night, fell to the floor in exhaustion as the song came to an end. Everyone applauded and Khari could not stop laughing in between heavy breaths. It seemed every person in the municipality patted them on the back. Khari had never enjoyed being with the town this much. Even Louis' eccentric dance moves didn't bother Khari and she found joy in the silliness.

Sam helped her up as the laughter faded. The music slowed and partners were found. He and Khari stared and grinned at one another, forgetting they were in the middle of a crowd. Sam neared Khari and they discovered one another's hands and backs as they stepped together and began to sway to the music. It was difficult for Khari to breathe in his arms. She didn't have to struggle to find the beat or rhythm of the song. Her moves were natural with him as they swayed slowly together. The melancholy guitar that serenaded the crowd seemed to be played for them alone and as they continued to move together, Khari laid her head upon Sam's chest. Even though the song was several minutes long, its ending felt abrupt and disappointing.

"Well, you've improved your dance skills," Khari said, blushing slightly.

"I knew you wouldn't be disappointed. And now I believe I owe you a large amount of chocolate," he said, guiding her off the floor.

After stopping to say hello to Khari's mother at her beans booth, they finally made their way to Khari's favorite "Everything Dipped in Chocolate" booth. With chocolate covered berries and crackers in hand, it was a relief to Khari to finally shake her restlessness from the past weeks and to simply savor the evening.

The square was lit by the moon, which chaperoned the lanterns dangling overhead like multicolored stars. While waiting for the anticipated fireworks display, the children danced around the crowd, each with sparklers placed in one of their tiny hands, a variety of half melted treats on sticks in the other. Their sparklers carved out trailing images through the air that gave the appearance of glowing streamers from nearing fires. Popping filled the atmosphere as tiny firecrackers emerged from youthful pockets and were purposefully tossed to the ground, exploding immediately on contact. The aroma of cotton candy and powdered cakes wafted from one direction, while barbecued meat and honeyed beans drifted from another, combining gently into one heavenly scent.

Khari couldn't recall the last time she had enjoyed the festival so much. She knew this night was a copy from every year before, but it felt fresh and unruly. Details were heightened, lifting her spirits. There was something different in the mix and she was sure that it was the peace that had somehow grown inside of her.

Resting on a bench under the gleaming lights and a full tree that hovered over them like a large umbrella, Khari and Sam finished their chocolate creations. Khari held her plate in one hand while she eased the fruit off the stick and into her mouth.

"See, my arm is completely healed. I can still eat from a stick," Khari laughed.

"I think you're more graceful than I ever hope to

be," he said as his graham cracker slipped from his plate and landed on the pavement, breaking into a chocolate heap on the ground.

Khari sucked in a piece of raspberry as she laughed at the clumsy sight, and coughed uncontrollably for several moments. As he joined in the laughing, Sam slapped Khari's back sympathetically trying to calm her choking.

"Hey! What's so funny?" came a voice above them.

Khari let out one more cough before looking up and seeing Sheffield arm in arm with a blonde—gentle and innocent looking. Khari guessed this must be the girl-friend he had told her about in the grocery store.

"Hey, Sheffield, good to see you," Sam said, half standing and giving him a hearty handshake.

"How are you?" Khari cleared her throat as her choking dwindled.

"It's a perfect night, isn't it?" Sheffield smiled.

Khari was sure she had never seen him with such a big grin.

"It is," Khari replied, returning the smile. She lifted her last stick from her plate, ate the final grape and wondered if Sheffield would take his eyes off the girl long enough to introduce her. Instead, he squeezed his arm tighter around her, smiling aimlessly into the side of her face. The girl looked embarrassed at his attention, turned a shade of pink and began gazing at her feet.

Khari and Sam exchanged grins, wondering what they should say to him.

Sam stood again and shook her hand.

"Hi. I'm Sam. It's nice to meet you."

"I'm sorry. I forgot to introduce you. This is the lovely Amy. My new *fiancé*," he finally declared.

"Oh, congratulations!" Khari and Sam chimed in unison.

Khari had never seen Sheffield so giddy.

"Nice to meet you." The girl smiled as Sheffield pulled her in closer.

"So, do you live nearby, Amy?" Khari asked, trying to keep the conversation flowing.

"I live in a town called Boulder which is about an hour south. Although, I'll move here once we're married." She shot a glance at Sheffield and he responded by touching his forehead to hers. They seemed to forget, once again, that they weren't alone.

"Well, we'll be excited to have you in town. You're lucky to be marrying Sheffield. He's always been good to those around him," Sam added, biting into his last strawberry and tossing the plate into the garbage.

"So, how about you guys? Are you an item again?" Sheffield inquired, sending a knot into Khari's middle. She felt the blood drain out of her. She had managed to avoid humiliation from her uncle, only to be ambushed by Sheffield.

"Well we're just...enjoying one another's company wouldn't you say, Khari?" Sam responded, flashing a smile Khari's way and obviously finding the whole conversation funny.

"Hey, I heard what happened to you, Khari. It was one of the most exciting things that has ever happened in this town, besides the time Margaret Faye accidentally poisoned herself with rat pellets. Remember that? The way her eye twitched forever after?"

Khari wanted to get up and run south. Sam, on the other hand, still looked completely comfortable and humored by the conversation as he leaned back in the bench and crossed his leg over the other.

"Anyway, we're glad you're all right. Did that guy you dated in England find out? I mean, I'm sure if he had he would've come to see you right away."

"Sheffield, I don't really want to..." Khari searched for some kind words.

"We're all happy Khari's okay," Sam said placing his hand on her back.

After a few moments of silence, the scent of popcorn filled the air and Sheffield responded to it immediately.

"It's time for popcorn. We better go get ready, Amy. I want to find a nice spot on the grass. It was nice to see you."

Popcorn signaled the start of the fireworks. They started popping it thirty minutes before the first burst of color; a signal for everyone to finish up with games and food and get ready for the show.

"Yeah, we should probably go get some dinner now that our dessert is gone," Sam chuckled.

"Nice to meet you," Amy said as they walked away.

"You, too," Khari and Sam responded together.

Khari tucked her hair nervously behind her ear and hoped the silence that hung in the air wouldn't last too long. She finally spoke.

"I'm sorry, Sam. I wish I didn't feel so awkward about this. I..."

"It's all right Khari. You don't owe me any explanations, really." He rested his elbow against the armrest of the bench. "I'm the one who should apologize. It has been an amazing day with you and I don't want to ruin it, but I need to say something that I've tried to say a million times before, but the words just never sounded right. When you left for England, I wanted to call you and write letters, but nothing felt right. Now here you are and I still don't know what to say."

Khari's heart sank somewhat at the uneasy look in his countenance and she threw her plate into the garbage next to them before she straightened herself taller, readying her spirit for a blow.

"What is it?" Khari questioned, feeling queasy.

He hesitated a moment before speaking.

"I don't expect you to ever forgive me. I'm not sure anything I say can express how awful I feel for the way I treated you a year ago. It wasn't the way a friend should treat another friend, especially someone I thought of as more than that." He paused for a moment and placed his hands on top of his head and gazed at the darkened sky.

"I should've supported you in your dreams and not passed judgments on you. I should've been there for you no matter what. For that, I'm truly sorry." He continued, "The last night we were together before you left, I felt awful. Deep inside I wanted to return to you and make it better between us, but my pride got in the way. I was so angry that you were leaving. And then I heard you were dating that guy in England and I was sure I had lost my chance. It was torture." He finally turned to Khari and looked her in the eyes. "I don't know if you still have feelings for that guy, but I need you to at least know how I feel."

Khari was speechless at the hovering words that now graced her ears. Finally talking about what had happened felt like exhaling after holding her breath for a decade. Khari paused and gathered herself. She wanted to say the right thing.

Looking at him, she could see that all of his boyish features had disappeared. It was the first time she saw a man. She finally allowed herself to wish he was hers, that they were partners in this crazy world. But she wasn't normal like Sheffield. She wasn't thinking about marriage or college and she couldn't act normal with the constant pull in her middle. It wasn't fair to Sam. It would be too scary to try again. Getting over him was the hardest thing she had ever gone through and she wasn't sure she could risk it. But just as she was about to tell him how she felt, she gazed in his eyes and suddenly all of her doubts disappeared and she said the only thing she could muster, "It's only been you..."

A few bright colored butterflies gently emerged from the air and rested on Khari's shoulder. He lifted his hand to her cheek and spoke soft enough that she was sure it had only graced her ears.

"You are my dearest friend, but I feel much more than that for you, and I know I will never be able to shake you from my memories, or my hopes for the future."

"Sam...."

Khari was speechless and deep inside his eyes she found a sure place. She couldn't see the mysterious future, but she was positive he would be there. It felt secure and lovely. She wanted to tell him she felt the same way, and that she always had, but no words would come. Instead, she fell into his grasp. She touched his hand as he pushed his fingers gently into her hair. His lips touched hers as softly and innocently as Khari remembered them. She could hardly believe it wasn't a dream. She gave in, sinking into a familiar world, one that she never wanted to leave.

Chapter Eleven ✤

The fresh feelings of the evening lingered as Khari sat at the edge of her bed later that night. Vibrations from the fireworks still rang in her ears and the wholesome sweetness of Sam lingered on her lips. She savored every detail of her emotions and couldn't shut away the resurfacing images. It was only moments ago that Sam had brought her home, an end to one of the most sublime days she had ever experienced.

She hoped her newfound euphoria would help her understand some of the pages of the notebook. She excitedly knelt on the floor and slid her hand in between the mattresses in search of the notebook that she had left there. But instead, she pulled her hand back into herself, screeching in pain. A significant drop of blood pooled along the side of her longest finger as a long wound appeared.

"What was that?" she mumbled out loud to herself,

confused at the sight of her blood and the pain pulsating through her finger. She grabbed a tissue from her nightstand and wound it tightly around the top half of her finger, applying needed pressure.

Khari turned toward the door at the sound of her mother entering the house, jabbering away with Virginia as they brought in leftover food. Virginia said good night before the front door closed. Shuffles from the kitchen continued as Khari's mother finished putting items away into cupboards.

"Khari, are you home?" her mother called up the stairs.

"Yeah mom, upstairs!" Khari called back, applying more pressure with the tissue to stop the blood flowing from her finger.

Had part of the metal binding of the notebook come loose? Khari knew she couldn't push her hand in again and risk getting cut a second time, so she heaved the top mattress to the side with all of her effort. Khari shrieked in horror and threw herself back against the wall trying to distance herself from what she saw.

"Khari! Are you all right?" her mom called up, but Khari couldn't answer. Her chest heaved in panic, her mind a blank. She couldn't think of anything except for the image of what lay before her and what it meant. Against the soft white of the mattress, as real as the notebook that she had left there hours before, lay a sharp dagger in its place. The same dagger Catunta threatened her with before.

It lay at a menacing angle with its shiny silver blade

aimed directly towards her. Drops of her blood left a trail from its pointed tip to the floor. Khari reeled, trying to assess what this meant. *The notebook is gone...it's gone.* Her stomach felt like wet heavy cement and her body trembled. She wanted to cry out in an angry wail, but her muscles tensed allowing for dense quick breaths and nothing more.

Catunta...Catunta...Why did I leave it alone? She noticed the drapes blowing in the gentle breeze and realized she had left the window open. She walked to the window and looked out. The rope still dangled from the tree, but it was shredded and split down the center as if he had used a knife in the rope to descend to the ground. Khari couldn't believe her stupidity and wanted to be swallowed up by the gaping earth. She slumped into the same corner where she had cowered before Catunta weeks ago and closed her eyes in disgust. She dreaded telling her nearing mother.

"Khari, are you okay?" Khari's mom rushed into the room. Before Khari could attempt an answer, her mother spotted the dagger.

"What is that? Why is there blood?" she asked.

Khari didn't try to open her eyes. They stayed tightly together.

"Mom it's my fault."

"What's your fault?"

Khari couldn't say the words and they stayed inside her heavy and poisonous.

"Khari, tell me what's going on, please...you're scaring me." Her mother stayed still in the doorway.

"The notebook was there, under my mattress. I reached in for it and was cut instead."

There was silence for a moment until her mother stepped forward, lifted the dagger from the mattress and examined it fearlessly.

"It has to be Catunta that left it," Khari whispered, hiding her face in her hands.

"Yes, it would seem that way," her mother answered.

Khari felt herself coming around. Easing herself from her stiff position. She finally opened her eyes.

"Mom, he has the notebook." Khari could barely say it.

"It will be okay. There isn't anything we can do about that now," she answered despondently. "How do I know this dagger?" she questioned ominously, turning it over, examining every angle of the decorated blade. It was the length of her forearm and was decorated beautifully with blue stones around the hilt and was sharpened and shined to perfection

"You've seen it before?" Khari asked wiping tears from her face. "It's the same one he had when he attacked me."

Her mother slowly exhaled and closed her eyes as if trying to conjure up a painful memory.

"Yes. The night you were born, after I had cleaned you up and was preparing to take you to the hospital. Catunta showed up with this dagger in his hand at the front door. He was only a teenager, soaked from the rainstorm and with determination in his eyes. I was frightened and weak and I gathered you up and backed up into a corner trying to keep you as far from him as possible. But, there was nowhere for me to go. He walked toward us and I pleaded with him to spare you."

Khari's mother opened her eyes and gazed once more at the sharpened weapon as she continued, "As he neared us, and it was clear my pleading didn't matter to him, the song I had just sang to you when you were born was the only thing that came to my mind. It was music my father had taught your uncle and me. The song filled me with an understanding of who I was and who you were. A peace filled my heart and I was sure it filled his because he turned and ran from us. It's the same song I sang to you your entire life."

Khari knew the song well, it had always brought her comfort. However, having such a cherished part of her childhood connected to something so frightening sickened her and knowing there were more details from her past that nobody had bothered to share with her stung. She had no idea he had tried to kill her once before. She was deeply hurt. Her entire life she had felt so ashamed and confused about herself. Her mother could have answered so many of Khari's questions, yet she withheld them from her. The hurt erupted within her again. She couldn't stop it.

"Mom. You knew who I was my whole life while I struggled to understand because nobody bothered to help me. Catunta tried to kill me when I was a baby? You thought if you just kept all of these secrets I wouldn't grow up to be who you feared me to be. I get that you were scared for my safety, but it would have been better for me to be killed knowing my identity and being proud that I had purpose, rather than feeling like I was losing my mind. That's why I didn't keep that dress or stay in London. I was too big of a freak." Khari trembled as she spoke.

"I'm so sorry, Khari. If I had any idea that you were struggling so severely I would have told you. All I can do is ask for your forgiveness. I truly thought I was doing what was best for you."

Knowing her mother was trying to protect her still didn't ease the feeling of being betrayed. Khari was tired of hearing excuses and wanted to change the subject.

"So does the dagger mean something?" Khari asked, staring at the floor.

"I'm not entirely sure why the same dagger is being used against us. We need to ask your uncle to be sure. If the dagger means something, he would know. He was always the inquisitive one about wars and weapons. While I fell asleep on my father's knee, Louis continued listening late into many nights about the battles of the tribes."

Khari's mom stepped toward her and helped her to her feet. She kissed Khari's forehead gently. Khari cooperated and stood, but her mind was reeling at her mother's words. Changing the subject hadn't consoled her and she felt the sting of deception squeeze her insides.

Her mother spoke softly, "It'll be all right. I know you're scared, but we need to work together to figure this out. It's important that we work together."

"Oh, mom. I'm sick about the notebook, but worse

than that, I feel horribly betrayed by you and Louis. How can you expect me to trust you and pretend that you haven't been the cause of so many years of suffering?" As Khari spoke a sudden realization entered her mind.

She looked her mother in the eyes and whispered, "That's why you arranged for me to go to London. Not because you believed that I was an artist, but to continue hiding me away."

Khari wasn't surprised to see her mother break their gaze and step away from her. She knew it was true.

"Khari…yes that's the main reason I arranged for you to go. I had a feeling that he was close." She looked Khari in the eyes again. "But that doesn't mean that I didn't believe you needed to foster your art as well, it was just a way I could give you both a learning experience and safety. Please believe me and forget about what went wrong. We need to figure out what we're going to do next together." Khari felt regret from the lost notebook and hurt from the life discoveries. They formed themselves into a tide of disgust and anger, which rose and grew within her. The thought of that awful man with something her family held so dear and knowing that her mother had kept her naïve about important details of her life, made her feel like her insides were full of hot coals. She felt murkiness spread within her heart. Nausea began from the poisonous feeling.

"No, mom. You've left me to handle things on my own my whole life. I can handle this too. I'll find it."

"That might not be the answer, finding it. We need to make sense of it all."

"Of course finding it is the right thing to do! It's the only thing to do! I never had a chance to decipher its meaning or find out why Catunta wanted it. I've struggled so long alone, that's what I'll continue to do. *I'm* going to fix this, not *you, Me!*" Khari yelled at her mother in a way she never had before.

Her mother looked pained at her harshness and stood unmoving. Khari would have felt sorry for allowing angry words to fly at her mom with such disrespect, but hate covered her heart, blocking any remorse. She couldn't stand her mother's wounded gaze upon her.

"I'm going to Louis'," Khari said in a mutter thinly coated in ire. She had to go. She needed to leave the disappointment of her mother's face. She grabbed the dagger from her mother's hand and charged out of the house.

The engine of the old truck roared desperately in the silence of the night and the flash of its lights into the trees teased her with eerie shadows formed in the deep darkness. Khari wept bitterly, feeling desperate and confused. The dagger that lay on the seat next to her shifted back and forth as she turned the corners faster than she should have. She didn't notice how tightly she gripped the steering wheel until her fingers began to burn, but she still didn't loosen her fierce hold.

She couldn't drive fast enough to her uncle's place. When she pulled up into his asphalt driveway, the porch light was on and he stood in the halo of its light. Khari's mom must have called and told Louis she was on her way.

She stayed still behind the wheel, drying her cheeks, feeling half sick from the late hour and from her nauseating words with her mother. She didn't want to touch the dagger again and stared at it, working up the courage to do so. To Khari, the hate, anger and derangement of Catunta emanated from it and when she felt its steel, it was as if she was touching him. She forced herself to pick it up once more by its gilded handle and carried it to the front door where her uncle stood.

"Come on in, Khari." Louis held the door for her. She couldn't read his blank facial expression. It was obvious he had been shaken from his sleep as he was dressed in his blue pajama bottoms and white t-shirt. His hair was left untied and lay long, pieces falling in sections over his broad shoulders. Khari felt great angst and passed by him without lifting her eyes as she entered the living room. She could hear the faint sounds of a whistling teapot in the next room.

Nothing in the living area had changed since the last time she had visited. The money Louis earned from his sales company was obviously never spent on decor as it held a distinct seventies feel. The gold couch was made of velour and the drapes were decorated with lime green flowers splashed on a cream background. The carpet, short shag, was a soft orange hue. Antiques and relics, along with statuettes and blown glass figures, filled a wooden hutch that rested upon the smallest wall. But most important were his prized boomerangs, hanging across the wall where Louis now stood, organized by size and shades of browns and blacks. It was uncharacteristic for him not to acknowledge the wooden collection immediately when she visited, and his failure to do so now left Khari feeling more tense.

He spoke nonchalantly, "You can sit down if you'd like, Khari."

Before sitting, she lifted the dagger without words, offering it to Louis. He exhaled through his nose in an exhausted manner and took it from her. She was relieved to have it gone from her hand and tried to shake away the repulsive sensations it left on her skin before sitting down on the couch.

"My mom..." Khari spoke, finally looking at him. He stood with his eyes on the dagger, running his fingers over the black waves inlaid across each side. Her words faded when she caught sight of him. "Did she tell you why I'm here?"

He gazed up at her and rubbed the back of his neck.

"Yes. She's very worried about you and rightly so. You've been through a lot. We're sorry for..."

"What do you know about the dagger?" Khari asked quickly changing the subject. She didn't want to listen to the same excuses for keeping things from her.

He stared at Khari for a moment and then took a deep breath before he continued.

"Well, this is the same dagger that your mother and I saw in your grandfather's house a couple of weeks before he was killed and your mother believes that he had it when he came after you as a baby."

Louis placed the dagger on the coffee table and pulled a toothpick from a tiny glass that lay next to it. He sat next to Khari as she mulled over his words.

"So, it means death? " Khari questioned.

"Well, not necessarily." Louis folded his arms and leaned back into the couch, twisting the toothpick between his fingers.

"Long ago, a dagger symbolized two things, war and peace."

"How can something stand for two opposite things?" Khari asked, confused.

"If it was given to an enemy, sharpened and shined, it was a declaration of war. But if the dagger was wrapped in a white cloth when it was given, it was a symbol of peace."

Khari ran her thumb over her freshly cut finger, realizing now why he had left it for her.

"So he's calling me to fight?"

"Essentially, yes. He knows of your gift. Once he and his father had met your grandfather and found out he had the ability to hear the insect's call, they also knew it skips a generation and that it would most likely pass to you. Not only is he trying to get to the land himself, he also wants to ensure we never set foot on it."

"By stealing the only chance I had of finding it. We have to get the notebook back."

"I know there are a lot of blanks to fill in Khari, but they will be filled with time. If you have the ability to sense the land, you don't need the notebook."

He didn't understand how lost she still was at finding the land. She knew he was wrong. The notebook had to be important or Catunta wouldn't want it. She tried to steady her voice.

"You said you followed him after grandfather's death. Do you know where he is now?"

"Years ago he was living in a town called Huntsville along the coast. He was a sword and knife maker. They said he was the best of the trade. I'm sure he's moved since then. I don't want you trying anything on your own. Promise me. We'll do this together." It was difficult for Khari to look into his intense eyes and realize not only that she was failing at her calling, but also that he had lied to her. She turned away. She had never felt this way. It was like a burning fire in her chest.

"So far, I've done nothing but make a mess of things. I don't know what to do," she mumbled under her breath.

She needed to get out of there. She stood, lifted the dagger from the table, placed it inside her bag and walked to the door.

"Khari! You're not yourself and you need to listen to me. You must not do anything without me, do you understand? Please go home to your mother. She's worried about you."

Khari only nodded, not wanting to speak anymore. She opened the door and left.

The late summer calm was everywhere but inside of Khari. She moved in the quiet of the house, slipping her sneakers on by the front door. She had dressed silently in her jeans and white t-shirt, trying not to rouse her mother. When she had returned from her uncle's, Khari had assured her mother she would sleep off her anxiety and discuss things in the morning and she had tried, but thoughts of losing the land to Catunta sizzled inside her and she just couldn't wait any longer. If her mother and uncle had it their way, they would delay and do nothing, and she just couldn't bear that. Besides, they had excluded her from important details of her entire life and she found it difficult to speak to them.

The sun had not yet lifted itself over the mountain peak, which meant it would feel chilly out in the crisp air. Autumn was nearing and moments without sun held a noticeable drop in temperature.

Khari slipped her ivory sweater on last and slung her leather bag weighted by the dagger over her shoulder before quietly bolting the door behind her. She couldn't take the truck, it would be too noisy, instead she made her way to the main road by foot. It would take her about a half-hour to walk to Sam's ranch. She needed his help.

As she walked, Catunta's face continued to return to her mind, the one who had killed her grandfather and who had tried to kill her twice. He now held the clues to finding their land. He was getting everything he wanted. She shivered at the thought of him discovering it. She couldn't let that happen. It was her duty to protect it and she wouldn't let him take it from her. The burning in her chest returned with a new fervor.

In the stillness of the night, Khari could hear only the sound of her feet against the loose rock and the intense hum of the insects. She felt the warning emanating from their hiding places.

"It's okay. I'll be careful. I have to do something before I lose my chance," she called out loud to the surrounding trees. She knew what she had to do. With every step she took, their song seemed to intensify, making her quicken her pace in an attempt to escape them. Finally, just as she reached a fork in the road, they were quiet.

No cars passed at the strange hour and she followed the main dirt road in silence. She kept her pace until she finally reached the wood fence surrounding Sam's ranch. Just as she walked under the iron arch carved with the name Delayne, Sam's last name, the sun began splaying its rays from behind the surrounding jagged cliffs, staining the clouds light pink. An immediate chorus of bird cries emerged forcefully from the tips of the many surrounding trees. Morning was here.

She stayed on the path along the fence until she met a small dirt road marked with a solitary black mailbox and lined with thick bushes and pines. She quickened her pace into a run, feeling the urgency of dawn upon her heels. Not wanting to wake Sam's uncle, she cautiously found her way along a curved stone path to Sam's bedroom in the back of the small brick home.

His window was closest to the vegetable garden and stepping from the stone path and onto the surrounding grass, she tried to get closer to it. She could make out faint silhouettes of the vegetables in the dim light and tried to avoid stepping on them. Besides the vines that had lengthened and spread themselves against the bricks of the house and the addition of rows in the garden, nothing had changed since she was here last.

Sam's window was higher than she could reach, so she found a small pebble and tossed it at the glass. The stone left her fingers with more force than she planned and instead of merely tapping the glass, a small crack emerged and spread into the pane. Khari winced, covering her mouth with both hands hoping that when she opened her scrunched eyes the crack wouldn't be there. To her humiliation it still was. She waited, staring at the window to see if Sam had noticed. Only the sound of a distant rooster crying to the emerging sun was heard.

After a few moments, the curtains parted and Sam's confused and weary face shown through. He wiped at his eyes in a gawky manner attempting to focus on her. His befuddled look changed immediately to a grin at the sight of Khari. With one hand still glued to her startled face, Khari waved with her other hand. He ruffled his already wild hair and told her to wait with one raised finger.

After several minutes, the back storm door swung open and Sam emerged in faded jeans and was in the process of pulling a shirt over his bare chest. Before he could say a word, Khari stepped toward him apologizing,

"I'm so sorry, Sam, I don't know what happened. I remember tossing rocks at your window plenty of times before and never making a scratch, let alone breaking it."

"Yeah," he laughed, examining the window from the outside. "Don't worry about it. It's only a tiny crack. Strange though, I think I was dreaming about fireworks when the splatter of window woke me." He laughed, placing his hands in his front pockets. "I wasn't sure if it was the finale to my dream, or if it was real. I wasn't expecting to see you here standing in the squash patch."

Khari wished she felt calm in this serene moment with Sam. It was lovely being with him in the dim morning light.

"Is everything all right?" Sam reached out his arm and took Khari's hand.

"No, not really." She looked away towards the mountains noticing the tip of the sun peering its head over the now brightened peak. The beauty of the scene was ruined by her tumultuous emotions within.

"What's wrong?" he asked, placing her hair behind her ear.

Before Khari could speak, she realized that what she was about to tell Sam might not go over well.

"The notebook is gone." Her voice wavered. "After you brought me home last night I found this dagger in its place." Khari pulled it from the bag and showed it to Sam. He lifted it and looked at it with confusion.

"So, he came back and took the notebook?"

"Yes. And I need to get it back."

"Okay. How are you planning on doing that?" he asked with deep concern. His face turned immediately serious.

"I need to find out where he lives, and I was hoping you could help me get there."

"Oh no." Sam placed the dagger back in her bag. "I won't take you to the crazy man's house and let him finish you off. There's no way."

"Sam, I know that you think it's crazy, but I'm not planning on confronting him. I just want to find out where he lives and wait for him to leave his house, find the notebook and leave. I won't let him see me."

"Khari, you're playing a dangerous game and I won't help you do it. You know what will happen if you go near that man. You're not thinking clearly."

Khari's voice trembled in bitterness, "I know this isn't a game, Sam. Believe me, I was there when he tried to kill me. You have no idea how much I have thought, and thought about it. I try to relax like my mom and Louis tell me to, but then I'm awakened by dreams, and there are whispers in my head and an anxious burning in my heart, that no matter how hard I try, I can't seem to get rid of." Khari pulled his hands from her and stepped away from him. "I can't wait around and let what is in the notebook disappear if it can help me."

"Khari, I understand that what you're going through is intense and I wish I could somehow take those feelings away, but I can't. I also can't let you be killed in the process of finishing what you feel you were meant to do. It doesn't feel right to me. I won't let you do it."

"I have to do it Sam. I'm sorry. I'm going with or without you."

She lowered her gaze and walked away. The burn in her chest intensified.

"Wait," Sam spoke in almost a whisper, "I don't want you going alone." He hesitated. "I will take you."

Chapter Twelve ✨

The sun was shining brightly an hour into their drive. A hint of heated leather from the car's seats warming in the sun filled the vehicle. Khari wondered if Sam felt as stifled as she did, but she was too afraid to break the icy silence and ask him. Instead, she opened her window a crack to let in the cool air.

From the time they started off in the Jeep, there had been an uncomfortable stillness. For Khari, it was unbearable to be near him and feel so awful. She wanted more than anything to engage in frivolous conversation and laugh about some stupid memory, but frustration and worry lingered, keeping her quiet. Shame from coercing him into doing something he didn't want to grew within her. But she needed him with her.

Khari glanced at Sam. He was obviously brooding,

one hand tight to the wheel and the other arm resting on the door. He pressed his finger against his tight lips in an agitated manner. No words would emerge from Khari and she stayed silent watching the scenery undulating as they careened down the highway. The landscape was drier now and full of jagged rock and muted yellows of dry brush and colorless earth. Small highway signs dotted the side of the road indicating they were in Native American territory. She recalled the books she had read about other Native American tribes, how their beautiful lands were taken from them unfairly, and they were left with the least desired parcels. She ached at the thought.

The arid surroundings matched Khari's lack of spirit. She leaned her head back against the seat and closed her eyes, partly trying to escape the anxiety between them, partly from mere exhaustion. She must have slept heavy because it felt like only minutes ago that she had drifted off before Sam's voice was heard.

"Khari, we're here." She felt Sam's hand on her arm as he tried to wake her. She never even felt the car stop. She opened her eyes and tried to focus while she stretched her arms.

"Where's here?" She felt confused rousing from her deep sleep. It was the first time in a long time that she remembered sleeping cleanly without any dreams or voices. Sam stood over her in the open door.

"You slept for more than an hour. We're in Huntsville. Are you hungry?" They were in the parking lot of a diner. A giant sign shaped like a mug overflowing with coffee advertised the business to the passing traffic.

The sun shone high in the sky and they were once again surrounded by lush green vegetation. The nearby ocean manifested itself in the surrounding thick air. Khari was immediately vigilant and gazed through the parking lot into the positioned and passing cars, searching for any sign of Catunta.

"I should ask someone if they know where he lives," Khari said.

"There will be time for that," Sam said pressing her arm in a reassuring manner. "Let's get something to eat first."

Khari never tired of his touch, but it was impossible to enjoy when she felt disappointment emanating from him. As they entered the restaurant, they sat themselves in a booth in front of a large window painted with scattered menu items.

"I can't believe I slept that long sitting upright in a seat. And with you driving." Khari grinned sheepishly, trying to lighten the mood.

"Well, I tried to set aside some of my off-roading stunts, but just while you slept," he joked.

"I didn't mean you're a terrible driver," Khari paused, "just adventurous."

"Yes, I used to drive more erratically at times, I admit it. But, I've matured since then." It was a relief to see him grin for a moment before opening his menu.

Khari ordered something, more from a need for sustenance than a desire to eat, but the lemonade, turkey and mashed potatoes did nothing to soothe Khari's tension. The conversation with Sam was forced and awkward, neither one knowing what to say, yet both trying to find the words. Sam barely touched his steak and picked slowly through his carrots and fries as he glanced out the window occasionally. Their dour-faced waitress added to the solemn mood with her short questions and curt answers. The waitress left the bill, half throwing it on the table. Sam's face remained unchanged as he reached for his wallet in his jacket pocket.

Khari couldn't take the tension anymore. "You can leave now if you want. I appreciate you bringing me this far." Khari spoke quietly as she grabbed for the bill and began searching for her wallet inside her bag.

Sam shook his head and looked into Khari's face. "You know there's no way I would leave you here." He lifted the ticket from its spot in front of Khari and left some cash on top of it.

"Well, I can't keep watching you so upset Sam. I can't have you hate me."

Sam's eyes were covered in sincerity as he deepened his gaze upon her.

"Khari, don't you know by now that I love you? That there is no way I could ever feel anything less for you? That's why it's so difficult for me to do this. I know you feel like you're doing what you need to, but..." He paused, wiping his lips with a paper napkin and tossed it on top of his plate before leaning on the table with his forearms. "I'm not convinced you're approaching it the right way. Does your mother or Louis know about you coming?" His eyes were strong and unflinching as he gazed at Khari, waiting for a response. Her heart skipped at his loving words and she felt a surge of adoration in return, but she stared at her fingers in her lap not knowing what to do or say to appease him, just as she didn't know what to say to her mother. She didn't want this to be happening either, but the responsibility was hers to fulfill and she felt its weight upon her.

"I don't blame you for not understanding, Sam. What's going on is strange, I know, but I can't worry about what you think right now. I have to do what I need to do." Khari realized her words sounded harsh and she wanted to take them back and reword them. He was silent, gazing out the window.

"Okay, Khari," he said, not moving. "I can see that you're not going to give in and I want you to know that I will support you in anything you choose. I'll help you."

"Miss...." Sam motioned to the young blonde waitress and she sauntered over with her hand on her hip.

"Do you know of a man by the name of Catunta?" Sam asked.

"Do I look like a phone book?" the woman responded curtly.

"Of course not. We just need to find..."

Khari cut in. "We're looking for a man that makes swords. It's for his birthday." Khari motioned towards Sam. "Is there anyone in town that you know of?"

"Of course. I've passed that shop plenty of times." She checked her overly long gaudy fingernails, then waved off a customer asking for his check. "The shop faces the road on Irvine Boulevard close to the shore. Happy birthday." She strutted off slowly disappearing through a swinging door behind the counter.

"That has to be him," Khari whispered.

"Are you sure you want to do this?" Sam questioned.

"I need to do this. I need the notebook's help." The moment the words rose within her, Khari realized that the disdain she felt for Catunta was somehow overpowering her drive to reunite her people to their land. Her reasoning felt more like revenge and she struggled with the opposing emotions.

Sam rose from his seat offering Khari his hand. "Well, let's get this over with," he sighed.

They found Irvine Boulevard several blocks from the diner. It was a small street full of quaint stores and wood planked walkways. Catunta's sword shop stood out with its large painted sword across the front window. Khari immediately recognized it as the same sword that was tattooed down his face. Her stomach sickened at the sight of it. It was his store.

"Are you all right?" Sam asked, noticing the change in her.

"There it is. He's probably inside." Khari sank slightly into her seat, attempting to disappear behind the dashboard. Sam pulled to the side of the road and parked next to a tourist shop teeming with teenagers who were searching through metal sale racks of t-shirts hanging in front of the store. Khari felt slightly safer with the crowds of people moving up and down the walks. He wouldn't dare try and hurt her in a crowded street.

"What do you want to do?" Sam asked.

Khari paused, unsure of how to answer his question. She didn't have any details of a plan. She only wanted to find out where he was and go from there. She figured she would watch Catunta's movements, search his home or workshop when he left, and take back the notebook.

"I need to know where he is first. Then I can sneak in." The sun lowered in the sky while they sat for what felt like hours waiting for some sign of Catunta. The only movement they had seen so far was from the passersby, but nobody went into the shop. The place looked almost asleep.

Sam opened the door to the car and got out.

"Sam, where are you going? Please get back in the car." Khari pleaded in a harsh whisper grabbing for him.

"He has no idea who I am. Let me go in and see if I can find out anything. Maybe the store isn't even open. Stay put."

Khari bit at the end of her thumb as Sam shut the door and walked down the road from where they were parked, crossing the connecting street to the sword shop. He browsed for a moment in front of the large painted window glancing up and down the street with his hands casually in his pockets as if he were merely window shopping. Finally, Sam turned the knob to the front door and passed inside, closing it behind him.

Khari closed her eyes and tried to talk herself through her fears. She waited, creating scenarios of what could possibly be going on inside, what words were being exchanged. She tried to reassure herself that there wasn't any way Catunta would recognize Sam. She was panicked and wanted to quiet the noisy streets and yell at the giggling adolescents to hush and let her listen for the sound within the shop's quiet walls.

After too many minutes, Khari was about to fling herself from the car and toward the shop when the door eased open and Sam emerged holding a piece of bright yellow paper in his hands. She was beyond relieved to have him in her sight, but ducked down once again as he made his way back to the Jeep and hopped in.

"Well, I just got a fabulous price quote on a custom crafted rapier sword with gold inlay," Sam chuckled as he tossed the yellow ticket onto her lap.

"You scared me going in there," Khari said exasperated, but with a smile.

"Well, if we are going to get your grandfather's writings back we needed to do something. Besides, the Catunta you described wasn't there. I spoke with an older man behind the counter who said the maker wasn't in today."

"Did he say where he was?" It was unnerving to know that he wasn't where he should have been. He could be lingering anywhere.

"He didn't know, but did mention to another customer that he lives in a large glass home on the beachfront, almost directly behind the shop. He said he would more than likely be back in the shop around closing time in a couple of hours. I'm sure he's close since his workplace and home are in the vicinity."

Khari shifted in her seat easing herself deeper into it. "Let's wait then."

Sam tapped the steering wheel with his thumb to the ticking time of a non-existent clock. "Khari, after he leaves I want to be the one searching for a way into his shop. I don't want you anywhere near him. Agreed?"

"No way Sam. This is my responsibility, not yours."

"Khari, I gave in and helped you with the insane search for the man who not only tried to kill you, but who would do it again given the chance. I can't allow you to go any further. Now that I'm here, I'll take the risks, not you."

The intensity in Sam's eyes told her that he was not backing down.

She reluctantly nodded in agreement.

A couple of hours passed and Khari was having difficulty holding still in her seat. The sun had lowered in the sky and more people disappeared into nearby restaurants where trailing music trickled out of pushed open doors. Except for bringing back food, or visiting a restroom, Sam and Khari stayed watching the shop from the car. As the hour for closing approached, Khari knew she would be seeing him and she felt tense at the prospect.

"How are you holding up?" Sam asked, placing his hand on her shoulder. Khari grabbed his hand and held it tight in between hers.

"I'm all right besides feeling angry, anxious, and extremely nauseous." Khari smiled, squeezing his hand tighter. She felt so safe with him near. "I'm glad you're here. Thank you."

"I would do anything for you," Sam responded, before kissing her on the forehead. She leaned in next to him and rested her head on his shoulder. She felt herself relaxing and tried to enjoy the moment.

The sun finally set as a small man with a cane stepped from the sword shop, locked the door, and made his way into the fresh darkness.

"He should have been here by now. We can't enter that shop not knowing if he'll walk in or not," Sam sighed. "We need eyes on him first."

"Why didn't he come?" Khari asked, not bothering to disguise her desperation. Her outrage for Catunta escalated.

"Khari, we've been here all day and you need to rest. I think we should find rooms somewhere and come back tomorrow." He touched her hand, but Khari barely noticed. She could never wait all night and begin again when she was ready to burst from every negative emotion inside of her. She wanted to go to his home, but she knew Sam would never allow it.

"All right. But let me use the restroom first. I'll be right back." Khari left the Jeep and made her way through an outdoor hall with windowed shops on either side. The hall opened up into a circular brick plaza of sorts with benches and garbage cans meandering among fake trees in pots. It was connected to three more halls, one in each direction. It was this opening where, earlier, she had turned right and followed it several paces to the restroom. This time, Khari turned left into a new deserted hall, leaving an echo of footsteps behind her. Sam wouldn't be able to see her and she could secretly make her way to the beach. She only wanted to see if the lights were on in Catunta's house. The notebook was more likely to be in his private residence than in the public shop anyway. Khari exited the double doors and crossed the street feeling strange at leaving Sam unknowingly waiting behind her. She would hurry.

In between two identical brown-shingled buildings, there was a public walkway to the beach. Khari followed the grassy path and descended down the wood block stairs onto the sand. The ocean was calm and spoke a languid strain as the cooler air eased gently around her. The soft movement of the waves meeting the shore was now her only friend in the dark. She made her way down the beach and searched the houses that lined the cliffs. Besides the gentle light from the full moon, she was surrounded by darkness, concealing her from any onlookers above.

She passed two lit homes before coming to a stop in front of a tall, darkened house enclosed by black iron fencing. The moonlight reflected off its long glass windows, which were seamlessly connected to one another. It was the only house made entirely of glass. It had to be Catunta's.

As she studied the place, she could see movement on the patio. A person appeared to be standing in the doorway, yet they were moving oddly. She stared at the image, trying to make out the shape. It caught the moonlight and Khari could see it was nothing more than drapery being pulled from an open sliding door and tossed in the breeze. Her heart lifted at the sight of the gaping door. With the house entirely dark and empty, she knew she would never get another chance this perfect to get inside.

In between Khari and the elevated home lay large black boulders like a dangerous ladder challenging anyone to climb its jagged surface. Khari's anticipation at reaching Catunta's home overshadowed the pumping fear that rushed through her and she pushed her hanging bag behind her and searched with shaking fingers along the giant rocks for secure spots to place her hands and feet. Large knots and crevices covered the rocks, making it easy to lift herself against them and ascend quickly.

Reaching the patio, she lifted herself over the surrounding metal railing and stepped cautiously across the planks to the open sliding door. The shifting drape was the only thing standing between Khari and the darkened house. She paused a moment to catch her breath before slipping through the curtain. With her first step inside, the sandy soles of her shoes rubbed too loudly against the glossy wood floor. She removed each one and placed them outside.

It was difficult to see and Khari wished she had thought of bringing a flashlight with her. Instead, she pulled the long curtain away from the open door and pushed it tight to one side, allowing the intensity of the lit moon to brighten her way.

Aside from the sleek black leather couches trimmed with chrome, the centrally placed furniture seemed to be made up of smooth surfaced glass and expensive stone that gleamed in the moonlight. One wall held built in bookshelves, mostly empty, but decorated cleanly with white sculptures and a few uniformed clusters of books. The shelves were covered with squares of aluminum that became spotted with the gentle light. To Khari, the room held the feel of a sophisticated modern art museum she had visited during her stay in London. Surprisingly different from the dark sinister cave she imagined Catunta lurking within.

Besides the faded sound of rolling waves filtering in from outside, the house was full of an unsettling silence. From the lack of sound or movement, she was sure he was not there, but couldn't help stepping cautiously through the spacious room. As she moved slowly in between the fireplace and a low glass table, trying not to run into anything, there was a tiny flash of red that caught her attention. She squinted, attempting to make it out. As she neared it she could see it was a tiny red bulb pulsing wildly. Khari didn't know what it was and approached it. Then she remembered the last time she had seen such a light: on the wall of Simon's home on a small alarm box. She had set off a silent alarm and whom it alerted she could only guess.

Khari darted back towards the open door looking anxiously around her for any signs of Catunta. Suddenly, she noticed another red light across the room, high in the ceiling, which did not flash, but moved slowly to the side. The light was at the end of a small silent camera trailing her movements.

Khari grabbed her shoes after exiting through the door, barely stopping to pick them up. She tried desperately to place them back on her feet while still running, which sent her stumbling into the rail tearing a hole in the top of her bag.

Half throwing herself over the edge, Khari moved herself quickly down the boulders, snagging her sweater and scratching her hands and wrists in her desperate flee back to the beach. It was awkward for her to run through the harsh sand and she nearly fell onto the wooden steps when she finally reached them.

She clambered her way to the top, and, not stopping to check for cars, sprinted across the road and bolted around the corner directly for the Jeep. Khari opened the door and jumped inside dropping her bag to the floor with heavy breath, ready to tell Sam to get going when she noticed, to her horror, the fragments of broken glass in Sam's now empty seat. Khari felt an eruption of pain in the back of her head before all went dark.

Chapter Thirteen ✎

Khari woke to a sound that she couldn't place even though she strained her ears to hear it. The noise was raspy and sounded as if two abrasive objects were being rubbed together. Was her mother scrubbing the sink or running Parmesan cheese quickly against the spiky edge of the grater? *My mother must be cooking.* She thought of the pasta dish she was more than likely preparing, or perhaps the grated cheese was to top a savory tomato soup or polenta. What a comfort it was to Khari to listen to her mother prepare meals. She couldn't smell what the dish was and tried to pry her closed eyelids open. She struggled, but they seemed to be sealed and she was too weak to try anymore.

"Mom..." Khari whispered, "what are you making?"

The grating sound stopped and there was silence.

"Mom?" Khari tried to lift her head, but paused immediately at the searing pain shooting through it and down her neck. She groaned in discomfort and realized there was no softness beneath her. She was on a hard floor. Where was she? Did she fall onto the kitchen tile? But why would her mother leave her there? Khari tried to lift her hands to her face to rub her eyes open, but her arms wouldn't budge. They seemed to be constrained behind her. Why wouldn't her mother answer?

"Mom, are you there?" Khari cried out.

"I wouldn't recommend moving. You had a significant blow to the head," spoke a deep poised voice.

At the sound of it, Khari felt confused, but after a few moments was roused to remembrance and understood why her mother wouldn't answer: she wasn't there. But, Catunta was.

Despite the stifling pain accompanying each movement and the inability to open her eyes, Khari began to struggle with every piece of her, trying to set herself free. But, she quickly realized her efforts were futile as she was tied too tight. She gave up after a moment of effort and stayed still, trying to catch her breath.

"That's better. I was hoping you would be smart so that I wasn't forced to speed up the inevitable. If you listen well and do as you're told, I might ease up on you." Khari heard his footsteps near her and felt his finger against her cheek. She yanked her face as far away from him as she could. *Where was Sam?*

"Sam!" she screamed. "Sam! Are you here?"

"There's no reason to yell, Khari. Although he is close to you, he can't hear you."

"What did you do?" Khari asked disgustedly.

"What did *I* do? I believe *you* brought him here, Kharishma."

"My name is Khari to you." She couldn't care less about correcting the usage of her name in this moment, but it was poison hearing him utter it the way her mother always had.

"Hmm. I could have sworn your mother gave you that name because it meant miracle. You *were* born lifeless, so the name makes sense. But, I don't understand why she did you the disservice of not giving you a tribal name. You are, after all, proving to be very important to our people," he snickered.

It angered Khari to hear him speak personal things about her, things that she didn't want to be tainted with his polluted tongue. She kept quiet, hoping if she didn't let him know it was bothering her he wouldn't continue. Yet he did.

"I wonder why your mother never told you about who you are. Do you think she was ashamed of the disgusting way you linger with the insects?" He spoke over her in such a way that made her feel trivial. She tried not to let his comments in, but somehow her eyes being covered only intensified her hearing and she couldn't escape his stinging words.

"I can only imagine how awful it must have felt to grow up thinking you were a freak. I guess I can understand why you would run away to Britain. You would have been wise to stay there."

He must have placed some kind of listening device inside her home. How else would he know so much?

Khari could stay silent no longer. He had cut her to the very center in every way.

"You don't know me Catunta, but it's easy to understand how you would be so arrogant as to think you do. Murderers are usually deranged."

He chuckled. "It's true that we killed your grandfather, I don't deny it. Your loyal uncle tried hard to prove it, but in the end I'm sure he realized what a lost cause his father really was."

"You have no idea what you're talking about," Khari retorted.

Catunta's footsteps trailed back to where she had heard the sound of grating and then returned to her side.

"Enough of the idle chit chat. If you want to save yourself, *and* him, you had better decide to help me. Thank you for returning my dagger. It needed a good sharpening." Khari felt cold steel against her face and the cloth that was tight around her head fell from her eyes. She blinked, trying to adjust her blurred vision.

It only took a moment for her to see in the partial light. It was difficult not to sob in anguish as she stared directly into the bruised and swollen face of Sam, bound just as she was, both hands and feet, a red cloth covering his eyes. He was lying helplessly on a now dried patch of blood encircling his face. Besides the faint breath escaping his scratched lips, he made no movements. Khari whispered his name repeatedly, desperate for him to rouse.

Directly behind Sam, Catunta's large silhouette moved to the opposite side of the room to a large metal door. He pressed several numbered buttons on a keypad next to the door and pushed it open. "He won't be waking anytime soon. He took a beating trying to fight me off. He's possibly as stubborn as you are," he said, his voice full of malice. "I'll be back. Think about cooperating for both your sakes."

He closed the door with a deep clang behind him leaving an unsettling silence in the small unfeeling room.

Khari ached and wished for a way to free herself to care for Sam, but it was no use, she was bound too tightly. She closed her eyes wishing for it to be a bad dream.

"Sam, please answer me. Please wake up." Desperate tears ran from her eyes leaving a tiny puddle on the cool floor under her cheek. "I've made such a mess of things."

She shifted herself nearer to Sam until her chest met his and she could feel his faint breath against her cheek. Watching him so battered she deeply regretted leading them directly into Catunta's grasp. He had probably counted on her to come after him. She had truly underestimated him. She had been so blind.

"Oh Sam! I'm so sorry," she whispered, nuzzling her face into his cheek. "I should've listened to you and been more cautious. Forgive me. I did this to you," she sobbed quietly. "You were right, I shouldn't have gone to London. I chose that path for all the wrong reasons and I knew it, deep down I knew it. I was afraid of who I was and wanted to escape the strange stinging inside of me, instead of dealing with it. Oh, I'm sorry for pushing you away! I should have told you I loved you, but I didn't. I do love you, Sam. Please wake up."

Khari cried and breathed along with him for hours, never giving up her quiet whispers to coax him awake, even though he never did. Finally, willing to try for an escape, she lifted her head slowly amid the strikes of dull pain and glanced around in the soft light.

The walls were lined with what appeared to be a dark red fabric covered with a variety of swords and knives, each showcased on heavy metal hooks. It appeared to Khari that Catunta had left them in a large safe that housed these precious items. She rolled onto her tied hands to see what was behind her. The room was the same all around except for the small camera in the high corner, watching them like a predator ready to strike. Khari rolled back to her side facing Sam, wanting to hide from it, realizing there was no way out. This room was chosen for its heightened security, lack of windows, and controlled door.

Khari was grateful at least for the life-giving air that had been leaking continuously from a dark vent in the ceiling. If only she could reach it, maybe they could escape through it if Sam would rouse. She had no idea if Catunta was watching, or when he would return, but she needed to at least try.

She sat up and inched herself around to the back of Sam. Lining her hands up with his, she began feeling for the ends of the thin rope that secured his wrists. Upon finding them, she fumbled for the knot and began working it apart with her fingers. The knot was stiff and taut and it took what seemed like hundreds of tries before it loosened enough for her to untie and remove it. At last it came undone and Khari felt a glimmer of hope. Next, she shimmied quickly toward his feet, working on the knot around his ankles. Just as she began the daunting process of removing the tight rope, the subtle rush of air from above was suddenly quiet. She worked faster trying to free his feet and felt a great satisfaction at the loosened rope falling to the floor. Khari then scooted to the front of Sam and lifted the thin cloth from his eyes revealing swollen skin around one eye and a deep scratch over the other. It was sickening to see him in such bad shape. He needed help, but he had to wake up first.

"Sam. Sam, please wake up." She spoke in a hushed voice and kissed his cheek gently, longing for him to talk to her. But after quite some time with no airflow, Khari could barely speak anymore and began to feel tired and weak. The oxygen supply was depleted already and she knew she needed to stay still in an attempt to conserve it. If only Sam would wake, he could free her and they could use the swords to defend themselves. She longed to see his green eyes and she lay down next to him, once again wishing he would wake.

Khari's breathing became increasingly shallow and she felt as if a weight pressed on her chest. In the escalating heat, beads of sweat began rising on her skin like dew on grass. She tried not to panic, knowing it would only speed up the process of suffocating, but her limbs began to shake somewhat which sent a flood of anxiety through her. Sam continued breathing faintly, oblivious to what was happening around them. Like a fish out of water, she struggled for air, waiting for the world to darken. Suddenly, the door pushed open and Catunta entered. A rush of fresh air entered with him, replacing the heavy soup that had surrounded them. Khari gasped and choked in the new oxygen.

"Well, Khari, you don't give up do you? Too bad you untied the dead man. He really is no use to you now." Catunta placed his smooth black buckled boot on Sam's middle and rolled him over to rest on his back.

"Don't touch him," Khari said with less gusto then she would have liked. She choked on her words and tried to regain her breath. She hoped her angry glare spoke louder than her voice, but he hovered over them without even a hint that he was bothered by her threat.

To Khari's surprise, Catunta was dressed in a light-colored polo shirt and dark jeans. It was different then the last time she had seen him, dressed in black and frightening in her bedroom. She wasn't sure which was more unnerving, he appearing to be harmless when she knew he wasn't, or dressing as scary as he really was. His raven hair was pulled back at his temples, leaving the rest hanging down long over his shoulders.

"It's time for us to find what we're both looking for. Be grateful you will at least breathe. It's more than I can say for your friend. Come with me."

"If you kill Sam, you'll be killing another innocent person! You have no reason to harm him! It's my fault we're here, not his! You have me, you don't need him!" Khari sobbed in desperation.

"You can't expect me to set him free and allow him

to run and tell everyone where you are. I cover my tracks," he said, stepping toward Khari.

Before he reached her, she secretly grasped the red cloth that had covered Sam's eyes. Catunta heaved Khari over his shoulder, hanging her upside down. She began to squirm in his arms, hoping to distract him from what she was about to do. He opened the door wider to fit them through and as Catunta stopped to punch the code into the pad outside the door, Khari dropped the rag, aiming for the path of the closing door. As the door slowly began to move, she lifted her torso to look at Sam one last time. As she did, his head turned slowly to the side and his green eyes stared weakly her way just before the door inched shut. To Khari's sheer delight, the door did not seal, as the tiny cloth wedged it safely open.

Catunta was silent the moment he removed Khari from the room of swords and into the garage, appearing relaxed, yet engrossed in thought. When he was tightening her ankles and wrists, the uncomfortable proximity allowed her to examine the details of his face. Behind the red tattoo that began at his hairline and ended at his powerful chin was a raised scar almost the size of the tattoo itself. She wanted to ask how he had gotten it, but didn't dare. His grey eyes, although intense, held a kind of despondency in them. In the moment, her hatred for him strangely disappeared and she felt instead, as if he was her brother, breaking her heart with his evil ways. She wished she could reason with him. But there was nothing to be said once the tape sealed her mouth and she was placed inside the vehicle. He positioned her on the floor behind the driver's seat and anchored her to it with more rope before throwing a scratchy wool blanket over the top of her.

As they left the garage and found their way to the highway, pinpoints of light shone lightly through the blanket's thickness revealing that it was day. Until now, it had been unclear if it was night or day, or even what day of the week it was. After being knocked in the head in Sam's car, it was unclear how long she had been out. Days could have passed and she wouldn't have known. Her screaming hunger confirmed that it had been a long while since she had eaten. She hoped Sam was escaping right now and finding help. It was torture being separated from him and getting farther away from where he was.

The roar of the engine was all Khari could hear from the backseat of Catunta's sleek SUV. They had been driving straight for some time before they began slowing and turning again and again, finally coming to a stop. It sounded as if Catunta lifted something from the floor in front of him before he got out of the vehicle. Although muffled, Khari could hear him speaking from where she lay.

"Thank you for coming. It's good to see you," said a man's voice.

"You too. Your sword is finished," Catunta responded.

There was a long pause before the man spoke again.

"It's incredible. It's just what I was hoping for. What an impeccable sword," he said excitedly. "You did an amazing job. Thank you. Come inside and I will get you the rest of your money."

Their footsteps trailed away and Khari was left in silence. It was shocking to hear Catunta being so civil and pleasant to someone. Why in the world had he brought her with him on business and where would they go now?

In the quiet of the car, Khari's thoughts wandered to Sam and if he had escaped. It was agonizing to think about him with his skin cut and bruised, lying with blood spread all around him, but it was even worse realizing that she had caused it. She spun her thoughts away from his face and his echoing voice that warned her not to find Catunta. *Think of something else* she told herself as she searched her brain for some peaceful thought. Instead she found the face of her mother, the way her eyes begged as she pleaded for Khari to wait. It was torture for Khari to think of the way she had hurt so many people in an impetuous effort to fight Catunta. She had even ignored the ancient ones who warned her to stop. Although the notebook was her driving reason for searching him out, she couldn't deny that her hatred toward him blurred the truth in her heart. Khari wept inside and wished she could darken the haunting thoughts in her mind, covering them as her eyes were now covered.

After several minutes, she heard footsteps nearing the car and Catunta getting in. The engine roared and they moved, at first slow and turning frequently, until once again the car rode fast and smooth as it would down a highway. Catunta stayed quiet through the whole drive. Only the rush of passing cars could be heard.

Just as her fatigue was about to overtake her, Khari

was suddenly thrown forward, causing her head to slam into the metal bar under the driver's seat. If she hadn't been anchored to the floor, she would have tumbled farther. It felt as if Catunta had swerved and pressed the brakes simultaneously in an effort to avoid something. The rope around her legs and wrists burned, as they pulled tight against her skin in the sudden movement. Khari was nauseated from the continual side-to-side movements of the car. She took in deep breaths through her nose trying to stop the rising bile from erupting in her sealed mouth.

The engine roared louder as they seemed to scream down the highway. *Why was he driving so fast?* Loud reprimanding horns blared around them, but his reckless driving continued for what had to be miles before finally the car seemed to slow and become steady once more.

What felt like hours later, the sun now peeked less brightly through the holes of the blanket and she knew darkness was near. Violent rocks moving under the rubber tires exploded and clanged against the undercarriage. Vibrations through the floor became more continuous as if they were moving down a dirt road. Khari lifted her head slightly to ease its uncomfortable banging against the unforgiving floor. They rode for miles before finally coming to a stop.

The crunch of the parking brake was heard before the hollow sound of two doors opening: first his, then hers. He pulled the blanket from off of her, allowing her to see clearly. She expected the brightness of day and squinted with anticipation, but instead the soft light of sunset caressed her open eyes. Catunta released her from the floor and untied her feet, but left her hands restricted behind her back. In one swift motion he tore the tape from her mouth. She would have squealed from the pain, but she bore it quietly, not wanting him to know it had hurt.

Khari tensed at the idea of being taken from the safety of the car. At least when he was driving he couldn't touch her. He helped her up and she cringed at the feel of his large hand through her sweater-covered arm. He finally spoke as he slung a long leather sheath, full of sword, over his shoulder

"I untied your feet, but don't try and run. You wouldn't make it far. You don't know anything about surviving on the land," he said as he gathered a large canvas bag from the front seat.

Khari understood what he meant. One glance around her and she could see they were deep in forest. There was nothing but the wild sounds of birds calling to the lowering sun and ancient towering trees hovering over them. Khari assumed they were going to camp under the stars until she caught sight of a small log cabin in the center of a small clearing. Khari was in awe at the sight of it. It was the same cabin she had seen in old photographs of her mother's. This was where she was born.

Chapter Fourteen

"Why did you bring me here?" Khari hollered, refusing to follow him into the cabin. It was too much for her to witness him invading such a precious place. "Why do you keep creeping your way into everything that's not yours?" she exclaimed angrily.

She could see him through the cabin's open door, and because of his almost complete silence throughout their journey, was surprised when he stopped his shifting around, turned, and stepped out steadily to meet her. He stared her in the eyes as he sidled toward her.

"All of this is mine to creep into." He lifted his arm and motioned toward the trees. "I have done nothing, but work and sacrifice for this day, unlike you who simply woke up one morning and decided to find some land because that's what grandpa did. You don't even know its importance. You read your grandfather's notebook as if it was written in a foreign language, not understanding the precious clues to an old world that runs through our veins. I am willing to die for it. Stop pretending you would. It's getting on my nerves."

Khari felt a sharp sting in her middle and didn't dare speak as he glared at her fiercely. His eyebrows crinkled with immense disdain. She could feel his anger and shrank before him. He was right. She didn't understand. She had struggled to decipher the simplest things on the pages of the notebook and from the insect's communication. Consumed with trying, she had ended up hurting everyone she loved in the process. Standing amid the grandeur of the beautiful natural surroundings, Khari felt tiny and insignificant. She was left alone and deflated. Catunta hovered over her like the many ancient pines and seemed in that moment, wise and brave, things she could not find within herself. She was humiliated before him.

Catunta seized Khari's arm and led her across the front porch and into the cabin. She didn't struggle. She had brought this on herself. Upon entering, she was hit by the dank air, similar to that of her attic, which filled the creaky place. Although the cabin was immaculate, the old wood planked floor and log walls, rugged and unfinished, revealed its age. He forced her into a rocking chair in the corner of the room next to an empty brick fireplace and untied the rope from her wrists. He then halved the rope with the same dagger that he kept hooked neatly to his belt and, placing each of her arms on the curved armrests, attached them firmly with rope.

Hopelessness and disgrace nagged at Khari like a fresh burn to skin. She kept quiet, not wanting to make a fool of herself again. Catunta made his way in and out of the front door, carrying in wood logs and other supplies and dropping them on top of the small uneven table in the center of the room. It was one of the only two rooms in the place, the other being a small bedroom.

Khari stared at the empty wall opposite the fireplace and although she was unable to distance herself physically, she gave her mind an escape, thinking of Sam's face. Not the battered one she barely left, but the distinguished one that always held a gentle exuberance. She found it and rested on the image. *Please let him be okay*, Khari cried within herself. *Please.* She sank deeper into her chair, not caring that Catunta would ultimately kill her. The hum of the insects was still silent and she felt utterly alone.

The sudden clatter of wood logs dropping into the fireplace ripped her from her reverie. Catunta began preparing a fire, which as far as Khari could tell, would be their only light in the tiny place. After stuffing crumpled paper into the open cracks of the wooden mass, Catunta threw a lit match atop, sending it into a quick blaze. The sun had completely faded, leaving the world covered in a dark shadow matching Khari's morose spirit. The birds were silent and only distant crickets and an occasional owl could be heard from outside the closed door.

Catunta poured canned lentils into a small kettle above the flames and stirred. The scent of curry and turmeric filled the air. The deep aroma soothed Khari, making her feel as if her mother was near. Catunta's features were only partially revealed in the orange glow, causing the red designed sword upon his face to appear as merely a dark smudge. She wondered again about his scar and, figuring she had nothing to lose, spoke in a lowered voice, "How did you get that scar?"

He tasted a spoonful of the pulse and clanged the large metal spoon against the rim of the kettle before laying it a top a folded newspaper at his side. He then capped the pot with a heavy lid, grabbed another thick piece of kindling, and added it to the shrinking fire. The touch of the new wood disturbed the solid flames and sent sparks jumping wildly to the floor where they dissipated slowly into grey dust. Silently, he prepared two metal bowls before switching the rope from her arms to her legs and sliding her chair over until she sat across from him at the rickety table. Khari assumed from his long stubborn silence that she would not hear an answer. But, then, he spoke.

"I didn't finish a job. My father wanted me to remember my mistake," he stated in a proud, but regretful, tone.

Khari averted her eyes unsure of how to respond and wished she hadn't asked. The horrifying image of his father inflicting him with a cut so deep that a scar formed was difficult for her to hear. Strangely, it didn't seem to bother him.

Although Khari's hunger was screaming through her, she felt more like curling up in a ball in a distant dark hole than eating. She picked slowly through the bowl, taking only meager bites.

"We have a long distance to go tomorrow, one that will require energy. You need to eat everything I gave you. I won't help you on the trek."

"Where are we going?" As the words left her mouth she wished she could retrieve them midair and return them to her silly tongue. She knew full well where they were going. The only thing she was unaware of was what he wanted from her and how long he would let her live. She was glad when he didn't respond.

Khari's back ached as they set off into the surrounding trees at the moment the sun's colors splashed through the horizon announcing its arrival. Although she was given a warm sleeping bag, it had administered little comfort against the hard planks of wood pressing at her body throughout the night. She had slept little and the rope, once again wrapped tight around her wrists, was beginning to tear at the surrounding skin. What little sleep Khari had, was filled with nightmares of a man with fiery hands who chased the shadows of her people from the white pine tree, forcing them to corners of a dusty world. *Listen, Listen,* they all repeated. Khari woke several times in sweat and tears, but after the final dream she awakened to see Catunta peering at her from the doorway of the adjoining room where he slept. The gentle glow of the fire brightened his face just enough that Khari caught his scolding eye. She must have been screaming in her sleep.

Now, amongst the trees, she struggled to keep up with Catunta's quick pace through the thickness of the green foliage. Khari was surprised Catunta knew where he was going. He paced with surety and confidence, carrying only a pack and his sword slung on his back. At times he would pause and pull a small canteen from the bag and share it with Khari, urging her with sharp words to move faster.

Khari's warm sweater, that she had up until now been grateful for, was now clinging to her over-heated skin and she wished to be untied just for a moment so that she could pull it off. Occasionally, while passing a bush or tree, the sharp branches yanked at its threads, leaving holes and snags throughout.

Khari yearned for sure footing and the ability to once more see the world acutely before her. She mourned for the missing connection to the earth and the ancient ones. She felt abandoned, even though she knew why they didn't come to her. She hadn't listened to them and chose instead her own way.

She stumbled several times. Luckily, her hands were tied in front allowing her to catch herself awkwardly on the ground. Catunta never slowed, even when she fell, but kept a steady pace over what seemed like hundreds of rising hills and endless sloping ground covered with fallen logs and mossy rocks. They pushed through the thick plants and ivy spread across the uneven forest floor. Khari's jeans were full of holes around her knees and her sneakers were filled with dirt and rocks, while tiny thorns poked wildly through her socks. Each step was awkward and clumsy and she felt lost and tired and increasingly irritated as the day wore on.

Several hours after beginning, with the sun high in

the sky, Catunta stopped and leaned against a large misshapen boulder. He laid his pack on the rock and removed several food contents from it. Khari collapsed next to him against the cool rock just as he threw a package of nuts at her. Her chest heaved and her skin burned. He held the canteen of water to her lips allowing her to fill herself with its wet life. After slowing her breath, Khari spoke to Catunta while he sipped at the canteen.

"Please...would you let me remove this sweater?" she panted. "I could move much faster if I wasn't overheating. I swear I won't run. Just untie me and let me take it off."

"I'm not sure how you're overheating when you're barely keeping up with me. You need to walk faster."

"We've been hiking for miles. You can't expect someone to walk that long without resting and be able to keep going," Khari shot back.

"Do you see me having any trouble? But if you think it will help us get there faster you can remove it. You might regret it. It's cold up here during the night."

Khari was feeling irritated. "What do you mean during the night? How far are we going?"

Catunta snickered as he gulped down more water. He crouched down in front of her and, looking her in the face, smiled. "Giving up must be a part of you, Khari. Do you see anything through? How do you think you could possibly be head of a tribe? You can't even hold yourself up."

He removed the dagger that hung on his belt and

began slicing from the collar of her sweater down to the cuffs on both arms. It fell in pieces into a pile on the ground, just as she felt her spirit had done.

Catunta picked up his pack and began his climb up the rest of the hill. Khari lifted herself to her feet, and with a new found coolness in just her t-shirt, once again followed him.

They continued on for several more hours, passing over tiny streams and hundreds of rocks and branches. Khari felt as if she were the only person in the entire world. The only comfort was in the vibrant scents of her surroundings and the sounds of the busy animals. She never tired of the forest's life and longed for the companionship of her ancient friends. Yet, they remained quiet.

It was nearly nightfall when they reached a large hole in the side of a high rock wall covered almost entirely by upward reaching vines and giant fat roots cascading wildly down from the tree that grew tall above it. The roots fell in front of a large opening. While the scene was picturesque, the place held a distinct feeling of evil that moved through Khari. She was leery at its entrance and a pit in her stomach began to tighten at the sight of it. She stopped and stared at the cave, feeling like it was a growling beast before her. Catunta had disappeared inside, but he returned when she didn't follow.

"What are you waiting for?" he asked impatiently.

"Wh…where are we?" Khari stuttered nervously.

"Does the royal princess need a red carpet rolled out before she will enter?" Catunta growled as he stepped out to meet her.

Khari tried to straighten her weary shoulders and approach the cave. She didn't want him to know she was afraid. "I don't need you to patronize me, Catunta. I kept up with you, didn't I?" She looked him unflinchingly in the eyes as she passed by him. She couldn't breathe as she pushed a growth of ivy to the side and ducked her head. Carefully, she stepped over a large root that lay at the threshold and willingly entered into the black void.

Chapter Fifteen ❧

From the moment she entered the cave, Khari sensed an unseen malevolence as dense as the gray haze of a smoky room. She couldn't make out the details of the cave's concealed contents until Catunta conjured a fire in a rock pit at the center of the space. It appeared to be a tiny makeshift home lined with ornate baskets of all shapes and sizes, along with colorful rugs and pottery. The entire space was just large enough that a small truck could be squeezed inside. Khari began to feel a bit claustrophobic. Even with all of the decoration, it felt more like a tomb than a cave.

When the firelight splashed onto the encompassing rock walls, black painted figures emerged. There was an obvious difference in the age of each one. Some were worn with time and others were darker and visibly newer. The men were similarly block shaped, yet varied in bulk and height, each connected at their outstretched hands like dark ink paper dolls. Khari counted each figure, ten in all.

Catunta must have sensed her gaze on them as he tended the fire.

"The men are my ancestors descended from Radaho," he boasted, "the first great warrior to be fierce and brave enough to take the land into his rightful hands." He passed in front of Khari and ran his fingers over the first faded man. Khari suddenly knew whom the cave had belonged to.

"His name was Radaho?" Khari shot back indignantly. "He must be the disgusting one who murdered the chief in cold calculated blood, leading to our people's destruction. I've seen him in my nightmares."

Without warning, Catunta struck Khari across the face, causing her to stumble to one side.

"I warn you to speak with reverence of my fathers in this sacred place. For centuries my descendants have come here, beginning with great Radaho. He was the one who tarried here first while searching for his lost land. It's the only sacred site left and the only place that holds the remains of the broken tribe."

Khari stood straight once more and tried to rub the sting from her cheek with her shoulder.

Bending slightly so as not to hit his head on the ceiling, Catunta walked to where he had placed his pack. From it, he pulled out the dagger he had come after her with, and the blue notebook. Khari's heart leapt at seeing the notebook so near. At least it was in one piece.

Catunta then crushed what looked like the root of a

plant inside a small stone bowl. It oozed black ink, staining the sediment that held it. He then pulled a long thick section of hair the length of his palm from his head and cut it easily with the dagger. He folded the strand and then dipped its ends into the sable liquid and carefully painted a tall figure at the end of the joined men, connecting its hand to the one before it.

"It's time to add my image to those of the brave men before me. Tomorrow we'll search the rising red rocks in the east, just as your grandfather wrote about. For centuries my ancestors have searched these grounds for any sign of the land, but never found it. Finally, our legacy will be fulfilled. There's only one direction I haven't searched in this part of the country. It must be there. Tomorrow I will find my land."

The same words which were uttered by Khari's own mouth just days ago echoed frighteningly from his: *I* and *my*. Khari saw herself in Catunta and shrank away. She realized, as she stared into his arrogant face which glared with intensity and hate, that she had fallen into the same trap, that she had forgotten about those she loved in order to find the notebook and land, both which she felt were hers and hers alone. Worst of all, in her selfishness, she had forgotten what the land meant and the importance of reuniting her people.

Catunta settled himself on the other side of the fire atop a bed prepared first with leaves and then a sleeping bag on top, which appeared to have been brought at an earlier time. Khari's bed was nothing more than leaves, but with the digging of the rope into her now raw wrists, and the nausea of her stomach, the poking and scratching of the leaves didn't seem as severe. He was right about the cold and she wished she had not gotten rid of her sweater. Shivers ran through her as she pulled herself closer to the fire.

Catunta ignored Khari as he prepared himself to sleep in the flicker of the smoldering flames. She was disgusted with the way she now saw herself and how similar she was to him. The sorrow in her heart, over what she had done and how she had acted out so selfishly, consumed her. She was glad she didn't have to speak to anyone.

Her center ached out its own cries of pleading for forgiveness from her loved ones and ancestors. Once again she fought to hear the earth and the ancient ones. However, besides the crackling fire, all remained silent. She knew why. She knew her mistakes. She wept and wept, apologizing in a quiet whisper for her stupidity and hate. She begged for relief and continued in remorse deep into the night until exhaustion finally overtook her and she was out of tears.

Khari woke to a tiny light streaming in from the opening of the cave. She lifted herself to her elbow to make out her surroundings, crushing the scratchy leaves beneath her. Matching her aching wrists was the ever-present sting in her soul, which still ate at her. She wasn't sure which of the two she wished would dissipate more.

It was her own folly that had brought her to her broken state and she recognized her guilt. She wished for her family and Sam there to help her.

With the glimmer of sunlight, a new hope swelled inside of her. Catunta was in the corner rummaging through an old chest. From it he pulled a colorful headdress and after removing an old red blanket and setting it aside on the floor, he brought out moccasins for his feet and tanned leather to tie around the tops of his arms. He removed his shirt and painted his chest and face with red and black root before adorning himself with the feathered crown and bells around his ankles. The strips of leather tied around his bulging muscles were last.

However, Khari barely noticed his preparations. Her eyes had not left the crimson blanket folded upon the ground. Chief Arankaya wore a red blanket in the visions she saw of him. Could it be the same blanket that adorned him? If it was, the white tree would be sewn into its center. She averted her eyes, trying not to call attention to it.

Stoically, Khari rolled to one side, turning her back to Catunta as he began a loud rhythmic chant. Some of the words were those from the notebook, which she had not understood, but as they left Catunta she recognized them as tribal songs. His voice boomed the words that left his tongue as if he was forcing someone to hear him. Louder and quicker he called. He had memorized them, but gave little feeling as he shouted each one.

Khari closed her eyes and tried to block out his voice as she attempted to create the words' familiarity once more in her mind, the way she thought they should sound. In her heart she once more begged for forgiveness and with each word she spoke, she longed for the ancient's attention. She cried and sang in soft whispers, smoothly combining the pairing of words together as she pushed her fingers gently through the ash floor, longing to hear the earth.

She focused and listened to the beat of her heart and matched it to the rhythm of the song. As she did so, the pain from her center faded away. Her now peaceful soul recalled the many times she had felt a part of the earth and its mystery. Even in London, thousands of miles from her land, she could connect herself to it when she felt close to its elements, removing the manmade world from her chaotic mind. It finally made sense why in her quest to find the notebook, she had lost the connection she had rediscovered in the forest. She had unknowingly pushed it away and replaced it with bitterness and rage just as Catunta had done.

The commonplace words she had read from the notebook many times came alive and seemed to beckon her as she relaxed and secretly turned an ear to listen. She abandoned her previous urge to dissect and figure them out. This time, she passed beyond the words to what was hidden within them. There was substance as they connected and floated into her yearning heart, as if she had inhaled them with deep breath. Pure understanding entered and she knew her future was sure and her person was whole. Her spirit was lead from the cave, to the cliff where the great chief had watched over the tribe, and to her wonderful surprise, he was there. The chief she had often seen standing mighty at the cliff's edge, always silent, finally spoke. What he said to her in all of his wisdom comforted and enlightened her. She understood the final piece to the puzzle.

"That's enough." Catunta's voice was indignant.

Khari opened her eyes, shaken from her trance. She had somehow risen to her knees. She didn't realize she was speaking loud enough to be heard. Catunta stood over her, still painted and in decoration, but now quiet and angry. Khari didn't fear him even though he glowered her way.

"You shouldn't speak things you don't understand." He walked over to the chest and returned his decorations inside of it. But instead of returning the blanket as well, he placed it into his backpack along with the notebook and dagger.

Khari looked at Catunta with a new clarity and could see how mistaken he was. He had convinced her that she was unimportant and did not understand. He was wrong and suddenly she didn't care if he knew it.

"You're the one who doesn't understand the words you chant. They're about the land yes, but not in place of love and brotherhood. The land is for the people, not for one selfish person to rape for himself. It can only be found when your desires are for the tribe, not for yourself. That's why it was taken from Radaho and why all of your ancestors were lost and unable to find it. They were seeking it for themselves and their stature, not for the good of the people. I made the same mistake Catunta.

You're blind."

He stayed turned away from her and she could see the muscles in his naked back stiffen.

"We'll see who is blind," was all he spoke as he put on his shirt.

Slinging his sword once more over his shoulder, he pulled her from the cave by her arm. Through fresh rain and thunder, they climbed for over an hour in an attempt to reach the top of a ridge, which was not far, just merely steep. When they reached the highest point he grunted and groaned, kicking up loose earth and pulling down moss from trees as he searched for something. Khari knew what it was and could see how far he was from it.

He stood still for a moment while Khari leaned against the stump of a cracked and fallen tree trying to catch her breath from practically running up the peak with him pushing behind her.

"Stay there!" he yelled. He then disappeared behind the thick terrain of the ridge.

"Gladly," Khari retorted under her slowing breath. Like a baby bird to its mother, she lifted her open mouth to the leaky sky to wet her thirsty tongue. She blinked against the rain falling into her eyes and smiled with joy. She could once more sense the life around her and knew where she was and how to return to the cabin if she could only escape from Catunta. The hum of the insects was thick in the air and she felt safer with their presence. She burst with pleasure that she was no longer alone. She always had the power to connect to the land, she just had to forget herself and listen.

Catunta had left his pack nearby on a large decaying log. Khari remembered seeing him not only place the blanket inside, but also the notebook and dagger. Before she could talk herself out of it, she quickly unzipped the bag, and with her hands still secured together, she clumsily found the knife. She would only have seconds to remove the rope.

She glanced at the trees for any indication of Catunta before sitting down and placing the dagger pointed side up between her lifted knees and rubbing the rope repeatedly against its sharpness. After several moments, the rope shredded and fell to the ground. The relief was profound and Khari let out an audible sigh. She would have rubbed the raw, blistered skin, but it was too tender and sore to touch. Instead, she blew softly on both wrists, cooling the burning slightly.

Catunta's approaching voice distracted her from the pain and she jumped up, dagger in her shaky hand, pointing it in his direction. She could hear him yelling and knew the anger in his face without seeing it.

"I DONT UNDERSTAND WHY THE ROCKS ARE NOT HERE! Tell me what you know! Tell me what the insects whisper to you. I know they speak to you! Tell me!" He finally emerged from the thick trees. Khari stood steady and approached him from the side, holding fast to the dagger in her wet hand. By the time he noticed Khari, it was too late. She pressed the sharp blade into his neck.

Catunta halted, his face dripping with water and frustration. He realized what was happening and changed his countenance into the insulting intimidator.

"Go ahead and kill me. Maybe then I would respect you."

Both of them stood, statues in the drizzling rain. The only movement came from the crashing thunder. Khari thought about the knowledge she had been graced with and it still expanded itself in her soul, allowing her not only to see her surroundings clearly, but herself and Catunta as well. She looked on his intense face and didn't fear him. Instead, she could feel their closeness and knew that he was her tribal brother.

"I honestly believed you were better than me, that I couldn't accomplish what I was chosen to. But now I see that you're the one who needs me. The land, our land, speaks and you know that you can't hear its cry. I saw in you the same mistakes I made, and realized why the land stopped speaking to me. I refused to listen. You could hear it, too, if you tried. You could see our land if you would only stop your selfishness. Greed and hate destroyed our tribe and I won't be a part of that continued destruction." Khari squinted, examining his face. "I know why you got that scar. You showed me mercy and had compassion when I was a baby and you were punished for it. At one time you chose not to have hate, it's not too late for you to choose that again."

Khari lowered the dagger and slashed through a bottom piece of her white t-shirt just as the rain subsided and a slice of sun peeked through the drifting gray clouds. She wrapped the cloth around the bulk of the dagger, tied it tightly and threw it at his feet. He only snickered at her offering.

"You'll never be a great leader, Khari. You don't know how to fight. And now, you'll help me, or you'll die, and this time, I *will* finish the job. Follow me. You're going to show me where it is." He picked up his dagger and, throwing the white cloth to the ground, walked past her down the hill.

Khari stayed still, watching him go. She searched for a reason to follow. He was going to kill her anyway, why not do it now? Even though she could clearly see the details of the forest once again and a distinct path to the cabin, she wasn't going to run. She knew, with the exhausting events of the past days, that she was not as nimble as she had been and he would inevitably catch her.

She sat herself down in protest and lifted her knees before resting her forehead against them and closing her eyes. She didn't move as his impatient footsteps rustled back toward her. She waited, ready for what pain would be inflicted. She didn't wait long. He grabbed her damp hair and pulled her head back.

"Get up and follow me," he snarled through his clenched teeth before pushing her head to the side and knocking her to the ground. He didn't turn to go, but waited over her for obedience to his demands. She lifted herself up from the ground, this time to her knees, and raised her head proudly. Again he came at her as his foot met her head in one swift blow that knocked her backwards and caused a light show to dance in her eyes. She pressed her head between her palms and rolled around trying to suffocate the pain with movement and was then met with another blow to her stomach. She turned over on her side, void of air, wanting to vomit and wondering if she would ever breathe again. She scratched at the earth trying to fill her collapsed chest with air. The insects were suddenly quiet.

Finally, after too long, she gasped in a breath followed by another and then another. She choked and heaved in the dirt and turned herself onto her stomach and waited, tears streaming from her eyes. She whispered to the earth and sky.

"I can't make him listen and I won't fight him. I can't fill my heart with hate. Help me."

She was unable to move as he lifted his sword from its sheath tied to his back. His heavy boots shuffled their way next to her and from where Khari lay so close to the ground, that was all she could see.

"I'm sorry, Khari, but if you refuse to help me, I have no more use for you."

Just before Catunta could lift his sword, a fierce wind began to blow, which lifted the surrounding leaves and dirt into the air. They swirled and danced ferociously about them and in a quick moment, a powerful hum carried on the wind met Khari's ears, followed by the ancient ones that came crawling to cover her. Thousands flew in from the skies and placed themselves delicately over every inch of her. She lay covered in a thick, soft, armored blanket of protection. Khari was amazed at the way they were trying to save her, but was sure their attempt would be futile once his sharpened sword slashed through them and then her.

She stayed still in the darkness, waiting for the end,

when the whistle of the blade being lifted through the air accompanied his deep scream. She was calm, anticipating the sting of the metal. Suddenly an object landed next to her with a thud.

What just happened? There was a sudden stillness as Khari listened for any indication of what was going on. She listened and listened, but couldn't hear anything. The insects slowly moved and once again took to the air or burrowed in the earth.

"What happened?" she questioned, while lifting herself up. Catunta lay on the ground before her with his sword still in his hand.

"Catunta...What...?" Khari rolled him over and could see a steady stream of blood dripping from his unmoving lip just as a voice came from behind her.

"Are you all right?" it asked.

Khari swung around to see a familiar face. He stepped toward her and lifted her from the ground. It was Louis.

"Uncle Louis? How...?"

"I've always wanted to use one in battle," he joked as he stepped over to Catunta and pushed his lifeless body to the side before lifting an intricately painted wooden boomerang from beneath him. He proceeded to wipe it clean with his shirt before tucking it into his belt.

"Did you just save me with that thing?" Khari asked, astonished that his quirky toys had proven to be worth something.

He lifted his large hands jokingly. "I always told you they were awesome. Besides, they're faster and more accurate than a silly sword. Sure they aren't as shiny, but I would like to see anyone throw their weapon with such precision."

Khari laughed. "Uncle Louis, I will never question your judgment in aboriginal weapons again." She tossed herself at him, covering him in hugs. "Thank you," she continued. "I was positive I was going to die. I'm lucky you found me."

"Well, it seems that it was more than just luck. I had a little guidance from your friends." He pointed to several bees and butterflies that had returned and rested on her arms and in her hair. Khari raised her eyes in surprise.

"It's true," Louis replied. "They led me here."

"I owe them my life as well. I am so grateful they didn't give up on me," she said as the insects once again took flight and disappeared into the trees. "At least *you* were paying attention. I'm sorry for what I've put you all through. Please forgive me, Uncle," she said, hugging him tightly once more.

"Forgiven, Khari. It's all over."

Khari felt so guilty about what she had gotten Sam into and was hesitant to confess, but knew she had to.

"Sam was with me," her voice quavered. "I'm not sure what's happened to him, or if he got out alive..."

"Don't worry, Khari. Your mother and I arrived at Catunta's place just after you left. We have Sam. He's in bad shape, but alive."

Tears of elation erupted from Khari and she sobbed into her uncle's chest. He held her tight, comforting her.

"How...?" she cried.

"When you left your house, it was clear where you had gone and finding Catunta's place wasn't difficult. Once there, we went to the front gate and there was Sam lying face down in the gravel. He was only able to tell us that Catunta had taken you before he passed out again. So, after placing him in the car, we drove to the sword shop and a man inside told us where Catunta had gone, luckily he knew he had some business to attend to and told us the address."

"He had a sword to deliver first," Khari interjected, letting go of him and wiping her eyes with the palm of her hand.

"Yes. We spotted Sam's Jeep with the keys still in the ignition, so I drove it and tailed you, while your mother took Sam to the hospital. I arrived on the client's street just as Catunta was leaving and I began to follow him. He knew because he sped up and just when I was about to head him off, he swerved and pushed me off the road. It took me the rest of the day to get towed out, but once I knew which direction he was headed I had a pretty good idea he was going to the cabin. So, after I phoned your mother at the hospital to tell her where I was going, I arrived at the cabin the next night and followed the cluster of tiny creatures to you." He smiled and squeezed her chin gently.

"That was you? I couldn't figure out why he was driving so erratically." Khari rubbed her wrists softly as she recalled the unpleasant car ride. "One thing I don't understand is why Catunta had the cabin. Didn't you sell it after I was born?"

"Your grandfather lost his cabin just before your birth in a poker game to Catunta's father. He couldn't pay his debt and was forced to give it up. Catunta's father always believed the cabin stood close to the ancestor's land and didn't want Tula to have it." He pulled a toothpick from his pocket and eased it into the corner of his mouth.

"Well, if grandfather lost the cabin, how was I born there?"

"When Cacha, your mother, lost your father in the car accident, she found out the day of his funeral that the cabin, a place that had been such a joy to her growing up, was gambled away to them. She was horrified and went there by herself. She was determined to stay and fight for a place that was so dear to her."

"And then I came unexpectedly."

"Yes. She went to the cabin hoping it would bring her comfort, but it didn't. She said it was just a dark lonely place, but then you came along and brought her the peace she needed."

"We have to find her. I'm sure she's sick with worry." Khari picked up Catunta's pack.

"I know she's frantic to see you. Let's get you back to the cabin where Sam's jeep is." Khari started to follow Louis, but her heart dropped at the sight of Catunta.

"What will we do with him?" Khari asked, looking at Catunta's lifeless face one last time. There was a great pain inside of her at the sight of him lying there on the ground. She placed the pack down and knelt down beside him.

"In all of his fury and anger I still found a connection to him, like he was truly my brother. I wish he had changed. I tried to tell him what I finally understood, that we were of one tribe. But, he wouldn't listen. We are just like the bees that began to die because they left their hives to find me. We can't survive alone."

Louis sat beside Khari.

"You're feeling the orenda of our people. It is the power between all of us as brothers and sisters. We are connected to each other and to the earth by it. It's unseen, yet very real." He breathed a heavy sigh. "I know Catunta felt that once for you."

"That's why he got that scar," Khari whispered, wiping the pooling tears from her eyes.

Louis lifted the sword from Catunta's grasp and slipped it quietly into its sheath now lying above his head.

One at a time she lifted Catunta's arms and folded them gently over his chest and touched, for the first time, the length of the mark from his hairline to his chin. She wept as Louis placed his arm around her. She didn't rush to feel better, but let the anguish ooze slowly from her heart.

After some time, Khari breathed deep, a new sense of hope manifesting itself inside of her. Once more she picked up the pack from a patch of pine needles and pulled the notebook from it. She lovingly touched the front cover.

"You have the notebook," Louis said relieved.

"Yes, it'll be nice to have the handwritten words of my grandfather, to learn about someone I never knew and the songs and chants he included. He's shared with us a few scattered hints to where the land lies. Other than that, it has no purpose. He knew the ancient ones were the land's true keepers and wouldn't allow it to be seen by anyone with a vengeful heart."

Khari reached in the bag once more and reverently removed the red blanket as Louis continued to speak. Anticipation ran through her.

"So, it isn't key to finding the land?" he questioned.

"I thought it was, but I was wrong," she answered somewhat despondently.

Louis walked toward her and peered over her shoulder at the blanket now in her hand. She unfolded it gently and gasped at the sight of the white pine intricately woven into its fabric and ran her fingers lovingly over the raised surface. Chills ran through her.

"Do you know where to find the land?" Louis asked.

"Yes," Khari whispered as she turned to gaze at him with excitement dancing in her eyes.

"We're standing on it."

Chapter Sixteen ⚜

The sun had disappeared completely and the trees melted into a darkened mass as Khari led Louis from them, to the front of the cabin. Surprisingly, smoke streamed from the tiny chimney, and a languid light brightened the back window. It was the only movement in the darkness.

"Who's here?" Khari asked Louis.

"Nobody came with me, though your mother knew I was on my way."

At the thought of her mother and Sam, Khari bounced onto the front porch and rushed through the front door. She felt strange entering it again under such different circumstances and her heart once more pained at the thought of Catunta.

"Mom?" Khari inquired timidly.

"Kharishma?" her mother's voice answered from the other room.

Khari followed the candlelight into the adjoining

bedroom. Her mother met her anxiously at the door and they fell into each other's arms and wept.

"I'm so sorry, Mom, for everything," Khari sobbed.

"Oh, Khari, I hope you can forgive me. I'm truly sorry for keeping so much from you. I was so wrong. I let fear make those choices for me."

"I forgive you. I understand why you wanted to hide me from Catunta. He was so driven by hate."

"I'm so relieved you're here. Let me look at you." Her mother cried while checking her over from top to bottom. She touched the bruise forming down the side of her face and examined her red, chaffed wrists.

"You sure are bruised and cut on the outside. How are you on the inside?"

"Better, Mom. Much better." Khari managed a smile before pausing. She was nervous to ask about Sam.

"Mom, where's Sam? Is he okay?"

Her mother's countenance soured and she stepped to the side allowing Khari to see the bed behind them. There under the patchwork quilt, fast asleep, was Sam. Khari could hardly believe he was finally in front of her. She stepped timidly and sat next to him on the edge of the bed, being careful not to wake him. She ran her fingers through his dark wavy hair and put her hand to his swollen face. She was relieved to see that most of his cuts had been tended to and no more blood was dried roughly on his skin. The red and purple bruises freshly wounding his face were now turning a green, yellow hue. He breathed slow and soft. Khari's mother stood behind her and touched her shoulder.

"He was in the hospital for a couple of days. They wanted him to stay longer because of his loss of blood and his broken rib, but as soon as he had the slightest strength to stand, he was out the door ready to find you. We couldn't do anything to stop him. After the long drive here his pain increased and he was turning a shade of turquoise and sweating profusely. I finally forced him to take his pain medication, which knocked him out completely. He's been sleeping for hours."

"He doesn't look well, Mom. It's my fault this happened to him. I was so wrong," Khari whispered holding his strong hand. She shuddered at how close he had come to dying inside the vault.

"It won't do any good to dwell on what happened, Kharishma. You need to move forward and figure out how to patch up any holes you've made." Her mother patted her cheek.

Khari knew her mother was right. She couldn't take back the horrific damage that was already done, but wondered how to help him. The hum of the ancient ones had been wildly intense since her time in the cave and once more she knew the land and could see its purity. She understood its heart and felt a deep connection to it. An idea came to her.

Khari touched Sam's face. She didn't want to leave his side again, but knew he needed what only nature provided. Khari headed for the door and removed her already muddied shoes. She didn't want any barriers between her and the earth in her search.

"Where are you going?" her mother asked in a voice

heavy with concern.

"I have to find a remedy to help Sam."

"Now? How can you find it out in the dark and without shoes?" her mother asked.

Louis interjected. "Believe me, if you had seen the way she led us through the forest. She knew every hole and rock. She'll be fine."

Her mother stared at her and hesitated. "Okay. But please hurry." She mustered a brave smile for Khari.

"I will."

Khari ran from the cabin in a full sprint, feeling the urgency of her duty. The sweet fresh scent of the damp bark permeated her senses. Energy from the many spots of dirt, plants, and trees emanated around her. Even the moss, although a gentler pulse, sparkled with life, showing itself to Khari. Each object radiated a different energy in varying shades and hues of colors, not necessarily all at once, but in cycles that came strongest when she neared them. It was something she didn't view with her eyes, but from the deepness of her heart. Somehow, she understood the purpose of each leaf, branch, flower, and stone.

After running for almost a mile, she continued, hopeful she would find what she was looking for. She searched the ground and above for anything that could help heal Sam. As she crossed through a small ravine, now dry from the rushing water that had once flowed within its walls, she sensed the pulse of a tiny flower with a dusty blue petal, embedded and growing fearlessly within a blanket of green jagged leaves. It would have been completely hidden to the natural eye, but it seemed to draw her in with its life.

As she neared it, she also sensed the danger of the green leaves, which almost hid the miniscule flower underneath its canopy. Khari was careful in the dark not to touch the berries attached to the leaves that surged a negative tone. She knew they were poisonous. Cautiously, she pulled several leaves from the mass to reveal the flower and once she was able to brush the flower's petals with her finger, she felt its importance and knew it was what she needed. It would help heal Sam. She apologetically and gratefully plucked the flower stem from the ground, knowing a greater power had guided her, not only to the flower, but also through the entire ordeal. She once again thanked the earth, sky, and beyond for their forgiveness and guidance. She lovingly held the flower tight inside her palm and headed quickly back.

An hour later, Khari rushed through the door of the cabin and asked her mother to make a tea from the entire flower. Her mother pushed an aged hanging kettle over the fire to boil water as Khari sat by Sam's side, this time removing the thick blanket from off of him. His fever was intensifying and could be felt without touching him.

"Mom, will you help me remove his shirt? We need to soak his chest with the flower water to heal his ribs."

With her mother's help, Khari lifted off his shirt. He was squeezed tightly around his middle with a stiff bandage to keep his ribs still. She pulled open the wrap at the Velcro edge, cringing at the movement it would cause within him. He slept on, seemingly unaffected. Her mother brought in a bowl of water, tinted green from the flower's stem and leaves now stuck to the bottom of the bowl. The blue petals floated to the top. Khari's mom handed her a white handkerchief.

"Thank you. Where's Louis?" Khari questioned.

"He went to the authorities about Catunta. He thought the quicker the better." Khari nodded in agreement and dipped the handkerchief into the steaming water and let it soak up much of the liquid. She rang out the excess into the bowl and laid the hot cloth gently over his ribs and replaced the quilt back over him.

"It will need to soak all night. I'll let him sleep, but as soon as he wakes up he needs to drink some."

Khari set the bowl on a small table next to the bed and then laid down next to him. She gently placed her hand over his chest and listened to the rhythm of his breath. From deep in his fever, Sam roused slightly. He weakly called Khari's name and tried to sit up. She stopped him from rising and whispered in his ear that everything was fine.

She gently lifted his head just enough for him to drink from the bowl. Thankfully, he was thirsty and consumed almost all of the liquid. Khari felt satisfied that he had the vital water inside of him and she was able to rest easier. Her mother, who was falling asleep upright in a rickety rocking chair, laid herself down on the sleeping bag by the fire. Khari once more positioned herself next to him and joined her slow breathing to Sam's. She slipped her hand into his and a song rose within her, the song that had been sung to her by her mother countless times. The words saturated her heart and mind and the tune flowed easily; an ancient song deep in meaning.

Khari sang into the night until exhaustion overtook her. It felt like forever since she had slept, and she quickly fell into a profound and much needed sleep.

Even the constant barrage of activity around and in the cabin as police officers scrutinized and investigated Khari and her family did not rouse Sam. After a couple of days and nights of dealing with authorities and trying to rid herself of the anguish of Catunta, she could do nothing more than wait as she and her mother stayed attentive to Sam. Besides a shower, the occasional meal and a change of clothing, Khari never left his side. They tended to his every mumble and twitch, concentrating on using up every last drop of the flower water and continuing with consistent reverent song, until finally, his stirrings were no longer in vain as he began opening his eyes. The morning sun was a mere afterthought to the brightness Khari felt at Sam's waking. She sat up quickly and held his hand whispering his name.

"Sam?" She brushed his hair back and ran her thumb over his eyelids encouraging them to open. "Can you wake up?"

He breathed deep and worked his eyelids up, squinting somewhat in the sunlight streaming from a nearby window. Sam focused on her face finally blinking his eyes awake.

"How do you feel?" Khari asked pulling the quilt

down to look at his chest. She rubbed over his ribs.

"How do I feel? How do you feel?" he mumbled weakly. "Are you all right? I didn't know where he'd taken you." He placed his hand on her cheek.

"I'm all right, Sam. I have a lot to tell you, but right now we need to make sure you're feeling better. Can you move?"

Khari held his hand and sat back giving him just enough room to sit up. He moved cautiously, more than likely expecting to be thrown down from pain. When discomfort didn't come, he sat up completely.

"Those pills must finally be working. My body doesn't feel like a bulldozer ran over it." He pressed at his temples with his palms and then searched his chest. "Where did that tight brace go that they squeezed me into?"

Khari chuckled at his surprise, delighted that he was better.

"Sam, you're awake! How are you?" Khari's mother asked as she and Louis entered the room. "I have to admit I wasn't sure you would be sitting up already. That flower works wonders."

"Flower?" questioned Sam, testing all of his body parts for pain.

"I gave you medicinal water made from a special flower while you were out of it. Here's your shirt." Khari grinned holding it out for him to take.

He lifted it easily over his head.

"Well, you have a lot to tell me, Khari. Let's start with when you supposedly went to the bathroom," Sam lifted his smiling brow at her.

Khari recounted everything that had happened, trying to leave out the more frightening details. Although, Sam, with his barrage of questions, figured out the horrifying specifics anyway.

"I'm so relieved you're all right." Sam pulled Khari into his arms and held her there.

"I'm sorry. I was so stupid," Khari admitted. "I did everything wrong, and I almost got you killed."

Sam kissed her softly on her forehead.

"I forgive you, Chief Girl."

"Let's not add chief so hastily," Khari retorted giving him a sour look. "Speaking of chief, I have something I want to show all of you."

With all of the worry over Sam she had forgotten about the Chief's blanket inside the backpack. She unzipped the pack and removed the folded blanket.

"This is a blanket that the great chief wore. It has a white pine embroidered on it which is an important symbol to our people." Khari passed it to her uncle and mother.

"Almost at the center of our land is a great pine tree whose needles are so pale that in the sunlight it appears to shine white. It's a symbol of peace. Catunta realized from grandfather's words that this pine tree was an important key to recognizing the land, but even if he had been standing at the tree's base, he wouldn't have known because of the ancient one's ability to hide the land from unwanted eyes. That's something he didn't understand and the reason why his family couldn't see the land. He knew the jagged rocks of the eastern cliff would point to the direction of the tree, which is where we ended up. But, he couldn't find the rocks even though we were right next to them."

"So, Catunta's family didn't recognize the land even though they had been living on it their entire lives?" Louis questioned.

"Yes. After everyone had been killed or scattered, Catunta's family was living in a cave nearby, but were blinded by the promise of protection from the ancient ones because of their selfishness and hate. It was their evil that kept them from home. It was the same path I had started to take," Khari reluctantly admitted.

Her mother passed the blanket to Sam and turned to Khari. Khari hoped never to see concern in her eyes again, but there it was.

"What is it, Mom?"

"Forgive me Khari, but I just can't help wondering what's to be done now. You can't do this on your own, and we want to help you, but each one of us has to take care of things back home. We need to discuss how to do this."

Khari knew the future was unclear, but was also sure that calling her people was the first step. After that, it was a mystery.

"I know you won't be able to stay out here all of the time and that's okay. But you're going to have to let me go to our land and wait. Now that the horror with Catunta is over, I can concentrate on what I know I have been called to do and that's to reunite our tribe. It'll be okay. I haven't seen much of the land, just the outskirts, so I still don't know what has to be done once I reach the center. But I'll handle it." She knew she couldn't do it alone, but after everything she had put them through couldn't bear to ask for their help.

There was quiet as everyone gazed around the room at one another. It seemed as if they were silently agreeing. Sam spoke first.

"I can gather some supplies and a couple of horses. Ember would love to be here with you." He winked at Khari. "A little work and we will have whatever awaits you taken care of. My uncle can do without me for a while."

"Me, too," Uncle Louis interjected. "I'll bring back some camping gear and food. I haven't taken vacation time in years. They'll be fine without me for a couple of weeks."

Khari was elated to have such love and support. Her mother grinned with tears in her eyes. "With some planning my assistants can take over the next two venues. Someone will have to cook for you!"

Everyone hugged Khari. "Thank you for helping me!" Khari cried. This was the first time in her life she felt like she wasn't strange, misunderstood, or alone.

"Well. Let's get going shall we? The faster we leave, the faster we can get back." Louis smiled as they began gathering their things and heading out the door. Sam walked slowly, still feeling weak. "Maybe you should drive," he said as they stepped out the front door. Khari grabbed at Sam's two fingers and held them. Sam noticed the gesture, "What is it?" he asked.

She looked from him to her mother. "Actually guys, I'm going to stay here and wait for you." She let go of Sam and pulled at her fingers, twisting them nervously.

They all paused and turned to face Khari. Her voice wavered. "As hard as it is to think of leaving you again, I can't bear to wait even one moment longer to get to the land."

Her mother and Louis shared uncomfortable glances until finally Louis stepped forward and hugged her. "Okay, Khari. With Catunta gone, we know you'll be fine. Meet us tomorrow on the ridge where I found you." He gave her one of his bear hugs and then her mom came from behind and did the same. "Please be careful, Kharishma. We'll be back tomorrow. It's only a couple of hours drive from here, but by the time we get everything taken care of and get back, it will probably be the afternoon, so watch for us then."

"I will, Mom. I promise, I'll be fine." Khari smiled reassuringly and squeezed her mom's hand. Her mother turned and hopped into her truck. Louis walked towards Sam's jeep and hopped in. "I'll drive you, Sam."

Sam turned to Louis and nodded in agreement before approaching Khari and wrapping his arms around her.

"It's going to be difficult to leave you. I'll hurry," Sam whispered.

"Oh, Sam, I'm so sad to stay here without you for even one night. You're so kind to even deal with me after all I've put you through. Forgive me, but I really need to do this."

"I want you to do it. I'll see you tomorrow." He raised his hands gently to her cheeks and kissed her softly. "I do love you."

"And I you." Khari touched his face, which was now covered in a layer of rough whiskers. "Thank you for always loving me no matter how insane I am." She smiled at him as they touched foreheads.

"I've never seen an ounce of insanity in you, just passion. I like passion." He held her close and Khari breathed in his honeyed smell before he kissed her once more, released her and walked slowly to his jeep.

"Bye," Khari whispered.

Engines roared and each vehicle began rolling down the small dirt road. Louis and Sam pushed their arms out the windows to wave at Khari. Khari waved back until they had completely disappeared into the cloud of dust being kicked up behind them. It was heart wrenching to watch them leave her even for a short time, but she knew it was necessary. She clung to the thought of not only their return, but also the return of her people, and it gave her strength.

She replaced the blanket into the pack and flung the bag over her shoulder, and then rolled up the sleeping bag and placed it under her other arm before closing the cabin door. All around Khari she could hear the many animals busily singing and the deep hum of the ancient ones. Elated, and anxious to discover what for so long had been hidden, she returned quietly to the trees.

Chapter Seventeen ❦

Several paces through a thicket of dense foliage just below the same cliff she and Catunta had been on days before, Khari stood silently in awe at what was before her. She could scarcely breathe. She was alone on the freshly discovered land and her heart pounded with excitement at the scene.

The late evening sun streamed through the lush vegetation creating a spotlight upon the multitude of rising mounds of varied sizes, which were covered in mossy green. The sloped domes were once their homes. Each full house was long and wide with a rounded roof and was big enough to have sheltered several families. Still wrapped in tree bark, long bent sticks peeked through spots of the jade growth and shown themselves as the backbone of the formations. Most were perfectly intact. However, one structure was missing a roof with its shattered frame protruding from the ground like the ribcage of a carcass, and the rest was in broken heaps. It was a relief that so many of the houses had been untouched by the fighting and fires that she had seen so often in her dreams.

Passing through such a sacred place, Khari felt deep emotion rise within her. The area had once been a safe haven and a refuge to so many of her beloved ancestors. She could sense the whispers of their voices and the joyful laughter of children at play. She felt their energy and songs. She was finally here. This is what she had been drawn to for so long, what all of the stirrings, dreams, and tugging at her heart had meant. It was no longer a hidden land, it had been found.

Khari approached the open door to what appeared to be the largest of the houses. She kicked at the web of branches and vines covering the opening, which broke and snapped at her touch. A few dangled overhead and brushed at the top of her as she crept cautiously over the threshold.

It was dim inside and more leafy vines covered the ceiling and walls, wrapping themselves around the high placed shelves and low bunk beds, which protruded from each side. A few animal hides still clung to the beds and hung upon the walls. Several empty and overturned baskets dotted the floor. In different corners, various birds and squirrels had claimed some of the space as their own and chattered and called as Khari entered. At the very center of the floor, several touching rocks formed an eerily empty circle, still waiting for a fire to enclose. It appeared that the occupants had left quickly.

Her heart ached at the thought of the fighting that had caused them to leave and scatter from their once peaceful lives. That same selfishness and hate which had once consumed her and Catunta, had eaten at the others as well and had led to their destruction. The memory of those fierce emotions again sparked the doom she had felt and she knew her people in this very spot had felt the same wicked pain. For a moment she could hear their cries of sadness and fury. Their faded spirits mourned their own loss. Khari felt a weight on her chest heavy enough to crush her heart. She grieved for them.

Khari stepped outside once more into the spilling light and made her way through the maze of houses, entering several more and discovering almost identical remnants scattered throughout. The houses were arranged in a stacked semicircle, each one facing west. She made her way through the skinny alleys their positions created, her tennis shoes pressing down a new path atop the green ivy blanketing the ground, until she came to the smallest of the homes. It appeared to be constructed the same as the others, just on a smaller scale, and would have maybe housed one family, instead of several. Khari pushed aside the green growth at the door and entered the home, realizing immediately that it had belonged to the Chief Arankaya. She could sense his voice and heart. She slid her shoes from her feet and placed them outside the threshold and dropped the backpack and sleeping bag on the dirt floor just inside.

She unzipped the bag and removed her grandfather's notebook and the crimson blanket. The only thing left in the house was a frame of sticks, which had at one time been a bed fixed and tied to the wall. Upon it, Khari lovingly placed both items and bowed her head.

"I am returning this cherished blanket to you, great Chief, and hope you will accept my offering of love and respect. I'm here to once more find and guide our people. My grandfather's notebook has helped me get here as well, just in a different way than I imagined." She grinned and sighed.

Khari gazed around in awe at where she found herself. She sat upon the dirt floor and, with straightened back and closed eyes, simply gathered her thoughts and feelings and breathed along with the silence, finding peace in her surroundings. With the sun lowering in the sky, she continued to sit and bask in the feelings she held and sensed around her, weeping for the past and smiling at the thought of the promising future. After some time a giant tug at her heart urged her up. There was one more thing she needed to see.

She stood and stepped outside the door. With the descending sun, the air was turning crisp and Khari tightened her sweater around her. Still barefoot, through the fading sunlight and into a clearing just beyond the houses, she searched for the symbol that she sensed was near. It did not take her long to find it, for just at the edge of the small village she at once spotted what she had longed to see, what had haunted her mind in a myriad of dreams and memories: the majestic tree, tall and untouched. Although it's needles were obviously a faded green, in the sunlight it shimmered white. It hovered twice the size of the longhouses, strong and healthy, and although it was visibly just a tree, it felt majestic and wise. It had witnessed so much. She fell to her knees, realizing the importance of the symbol before her and how much it had meant to her people.

She pushed her hands against the needled ground, sensing the pulse of life within the earth. She knew that this was the moment and the place to call her people. She pledged to use all of her wisdom for the good of her tribe and could feel the burst of anticipation grow within her. It was the very moment she had been waiting for and there was nothing standing in her way.

A tiny bee once again glided to her side and rested on her shoulder just before an array of other insects joined from above and below, surrounding her with their colorful beauty. They floated around her and the tree, churning the air with their beating wings, creating a whirlwind of heavy applause and flashes of color. Khari gazed up into their synchronized dance and laughed and spun along with them.

On the sweet breeze that they created, and on her lips, a melody rose and she called out inspired ancient words to the spacious sky and felt the presence of her ancestors at her back, guiding her thoughts and steps. Her feet rose and fell to the earth in time with the familiar music, which permeated her brain like a deep rich scent. Alone with the earth, now darkening with the setting sun, she cried the words, attempting to send them to heaven, relishing the knowledge that the earth and sky spoke back.

Khari gave all her devotion and strength to the natural music, turning to the rhythm, feeling the new language emerge within her, calling louder and louder with her voice and lifting her hands to the sky, feeling for a powerful force that seemed to come from every direction. Peace and happiness were on her joyful tongue.

The stars and gentle light of the moon gave her energy and she spun, pressing her feet and nodding her head again and again, connecting with the air that swayed against her. No part of her stayed still. She was in full motion, moving with the pure shifting of the earth and its elements, lost in a harmonious dimension. She knew the purpose of her song and dance and felt it connect her to her people from all distances and times. She called them to listen. She sent her knowledge on the air, hoping listening hearts and open minds would receive it. *Come,* she called, *come.* Deep into the night she called, *listen, please listen.*

Khari sat still on the cliff in the same spot Chief Arankaya had been hundreds of years before, overlooking the same land that was now awake and full of life. It was just as she imagined it was in the beginning.

It had been two weeks since she had sung and danced before the white pine and her heart grew restless at not seeing anyone arrive from her tribe. She clung to a drawing notebook, which she had filled with sketches since her arrival. It felt amazing to be able to draw and paint again. She held her sharpened pencil sideways and gently shaded a part of the pine now on paper before her.

With the help of Sam, Louis, and her mother, the space was almost completely clear of overgrown vegetation and the large fire pit was once again roaring and hot, filling the air with its rich scent. Khari came to the cliff each morning to look over their progress. She wanted everything to be ready and could see the longhouses were almost clear of the thick green ivy and branches that had engulfed them. The bark coverings looked fresh in the brightening sun. She marveled at the new fall leaves, oozing with new bright colors as if dipped in paint and hung on the branches to dry.

The river farther down was rushing and she could hear and see its winding path. Ember trotted alongside a brown mare through the many trees and ended at the riverbank to drink. Khari was elated Sam had brought them.

Sam exited one of the longhouses with a hand towel draped over his shoulder and a toothbrush in his hand. He waved and called to her, "Good morning Khari! How's the view?" Khari could see his giant smile from where she sat as he lifted his toothbrush in greeting.

"Better now that you're in it!" she called back, chuckling at his disheveled hair still standing up in the back.

He and Louis slept in one of the smaller of the longhouses next to the one she and her mother shared. It had taken days to clean out the many creatures, leafy life, and cobwebs that had overtaken the spaces before adding sleeping bags, lanterns and other supplies inside.

Louis was finishing up breakfast as Khari's mother slowly made her way up to Khari.

"Are you hungry?" her mother asked as she sat down beside her.

"Yes. I'm sorry, I just wanted to finish this drawing."

"And watch for any arrivals?"

Khari grinned sheepishly. "Yes. That, too."

"Don't worry, sweetie, they're going to come. Have patience."

"I keep telling myself that, but then days go by and we hear nothing and I begin to worry that I didn't complete something I was supposed to, or that I did something wrong, or that I am not trusting enough. But then I start to panic that if they do come, I won't know what to say to them." Khari sat up straight and peered at the clear sky. "Catunta mocked me for so many things, from my gullibility, to my name, and even though I know he was wrong about me on so many levels, I also know he was right about other things. How can I introduce myself with a strange foreign name and claim to be their Native American sister? How will I lead when I'm learning so much myself? I'm scared."

Her mother pulled Khari's hair from her shoulders and placed her arm around her.

"You know, when you were born, I felt exactly the way you're feeling now. I felt completely isolated and frightened in the cabin, especially when you emerged and weren't breathing. I had no idea what to do. But, the lack of knowledge allowed for faith to take over and then something miraculous happened. I suddenly sensed that even though it appeared that I was alone, I really wasn't. There was a power beyond myself who knew me, loved me, and brought me from my dark place, a power that guided me through the scariest trial of my life. And, although you don't remember, I know that presence was there for you, to protect you and help you live. It's still with you. You've done everything expected of you. Now you need to trust in yourself and all you've learned. You can't do it alone, and nobody expects you to."

Khari knew her mother was right, that there was an unseen force that had brought her there and that everything she had gone through had taught her more than if she had read it or had been told. She had to experience those emotions for herself to understand what her tribe had felt. She was stronger and she could feel it.

"Thanks, Mom." Khari leaned her head on her mother's shoulder.

"You looked cold, so I brought you this," her mother said, reaching behind her and opening Arankaya's blanket before gently placing it around Khari's shoulders. Khari stiffened at its touch.

"I don't feel like I should wear it, Mom. He was such a great chief and I haven't lived up to even a part of what he was. I don't deserve it." She tried to remove it, but her mother eased it against her shoulders once more.

"It's not about earning the right to wear it, it's about *honoring* him by wearing it. He's passed you the land, with full confidence that you'll fulfill what he needs you to. He gave you his calling. Wear it with honor, never forgetting what he stood for. Wear it as he would wear it: with pride for your people."

Khari smiled and squeezed her, enjoying her embrace. "All right. I will."

"Well, breakfast is ready when you are." Her mother stood up and started her way back down the hill.

"Thanks. I'll be right there."

Leaving her drawings on the ground, she wrapped the red wool blanket tighter around herself, enjoying the cool fall air. She closed her eyes for a moment allowing the morning sun to warm her. With a deep breath, Khari stood and brushed herself off and made sure the blanket didn't drag on the ground before turning to make her way down the rocky path to camp. Suddenly, she froze and peered toward the edge of the village at a man stepping out into the clearing of tall grass, just beyond the white pine and longhouses. He stood peering around him, looking a bit confused at where he was when several more people emerged from behind him, gathering and conversing. Khari gasped at the sight and wanted to run to them, but the trepidation she felt overpowered the impulse and caused her instead to freeze.

They were a small crowd of people, young and old. They moved in close together, and began quietly chatting among themselves. Khari stood full of emotion at their splendor. She felt timid at her task, finding it difficult to move.

Khari's mother, who had noticed their arrival as well,

gazed at her from the bottom and seemed to say with her dancing smile, *Go and meet our people.*

Gathering herself, Khari finally moved and descended the dew touched hill, passing by Sam and Louis at the fire in front of the cluster of longhouses. They both followed Khari's gaze to see what she was staring at and watched her step slowly in the direction of the group.

"I guess we'll need to make more breakfast," Louis said as Sam slapped him on the back.

"I think you're right," Sam laughed.

The bees were quiet in a nearby hive and the other insects reverently stopped their hum. Khari paused for a moment before reaching the group and turned to see her mother joining with Sam and Louis. They smiled at Khari and nodded their heads in encouragement.

As she neared the gathering, she pulled the blanket tighter around her shoulders. She could hear them voicing questions to one another, explaining how far they had come and sharing the deep feelings that had guided them. When they noticed Khari, their whispers faded into silence as each one turned towards her and watched her move their way.

Khari approached them, fighting back the fierce emotions that rose within her. The first man, who was young, built strong and tall, with kind eyes and short black hair, stood in front and spoke with a pause, "Hi…my name is Jesse. It seems that none of us know what's going on. We actually don't even know one another, but we all had the same thoughts and dreams showing us the way here. I know it sounds crazy, but do you know where we are or why we're here?"

Khari smiled boldly at him with tears streaming from her eyes and held out her hand, which he took. "Yes, I do. My name is Kharishma. I called you here. I called you home."

AUTHOR'S NOTE

I must acknowledge the beautifully written and illustrated book, *500 Nations* by Alvin M. Josephy, JR., which inspired several details in the story of Kharishma. Josephy's book gave me a needed glimpse into the fascinating world of our Native American brothers and sisters and a greater insight into the beauty of their culture.

While characters were fictional, the symbol of the white pine and the spiritual power called "orenda" were taken from the beliefs of the Hodenosaunee people. Also, in their legend, a war-craving figure named Thadadaho caused much death and destruction among their people. He was finally convinced to change and join a life of peace with the other tribes, by a wise man named, The Peace Maker. The five tribes of the Hodenosaunee accepted The Peace Maker's thirteen inspirational laws and peace finally reigned. My characters Radaho and Chief Arancaya, were inspired from these two legendary figures.

ABOUT THE AUTHOR

Jenny L. R. Nay graduated from Northeastern University with a degree in English. She lives on a little mountain in Utah with her husband and four children. This is her first novel.